Hell Squad: Roth

Anna Hackett

Roth

Published by Anna Hackett
Copyright 2015 by Anna Hackett
Cover by Melody Simmons of eBookindiecovers
Edits by Tanya Saari

ISBN (eBook): 978-0-9943584-4-8
ISBN (paperback): 978-0-9945572-1-6

What readers are saying about Anna's Science Fiction Romance

At Star's End – One of Library Journal's Best E-Original Romances for 2014

Return to Dark Earth – One of Library Journal's Best E-Original Books for 2015 and two-time SFR Galaxy Awards winner

The Phoenix Adventures – SFR Galaxy Award Winner for Most Fun New Series and "Why Isn't This a Movie?" Series

Beneath a Trojan Moon – SFR Galaxy Award Winner and RWAus Ella Award Winner

Hell Squad – Amazon Bestselling Sci-fi Romance Series and SFR Galaxy Award Winner

"Like Indiana Jones meets Star Wars. A treasure hunt with a steamy romance." – SFF Dragon, review of *Among Galactic Ruins*

"High action and adventure surrounding an impossible treasure hunt kept me reading until late in the night." – Jen, That's What I'm Talking About, review of *Beyond Galaxy's Edge*

"Action, danger, aliens, romance – yup, it's another great book from Anna Hackett!" – Book Gannet Reviews, review of *Hell Squad: Marcus*

Don't miss out! For updates about new releases, action romance info, free books, and other fun stuff, sign up for my VIP mailing list and get your *free box set* containing three action-packed romances.

Visit here to get started:
www.annahackettbooks.com

Chapter One

It was too damned quiet.

Roth Masters studied the ground below from his birds-eye view. He moved the controls and the Darkswift—a sleek, powered, two-man glider— turned left.

Not a single alien to be seen. Just the way it had been for a full week. Not that you could forget what had happened. Below, the ruins of Sydney spread out before him. Shattered buildings, burned-out vehicles, overgrown parks and gardens. There wasn't much left to tell you it had once been the beautiful harbor capital of the United Coalition of Countries.

He lifted his gaze and spotted the alien ship in the distance. It sat on the remains of Sydney Airport's runways. It looked like a giant beast, crouched and ready to dive into the water nearby.

Shit, he could hardly believe he'd been inside that ship just a few days ago. While he was there, he'd helped destroy the aliens' power source.

But while the raptor patrols weren't back out in the streets yet, he could see lights on near the ship. His jaw tightened. They were recovering.

"No sign of any raptors," a sharp female voice said. "Not even a lost canid."

He turned his head and eyed his second-in-command. Mackenna Carides was small, but tougher than the carbon fiber of his armor. "Nope."

They were both lying on their stomachs, with the heads-up display in front of them and the dark canopy enclosing them in the cockpit. He knew Mac loved to fly, and Roth, after a beer or two, could wax pretty lyrical about the Darkswifts himself. He wished he'd had them when he'd been a part of the Special Operations Command with the Coalition military.

Now, Squad Nine used the Darkswifts to infiltrate raptor territory and spy on the aliens, or to provide backup for any of the other commando squads from Blue Mountain Base who came into the city to fight the aliens.

Usually it was Hell Squad—the roughest, toughest squad on the base.

Speaking of which...Roth tapped the control screen. "Steele? You there? See anything on the ground?"

"That's a negative, Masters." The gravelly voice of Hell Squad's leader came through the comm line.

Roth turned the Darkswift again. On the ground, he spotted the six members of Hell Squad moving down a rubble-strewn street. They were all in black armor, carbine weapons up.

Off to his left, he caught sight of two blurred glimmers in the sky. The rest of his squad. Taylor Cates and Camryn McNab were paired in one

Darkswift, while Sienna Rossi and Theron Wade were in the other. The crafts' illusion systems were up, rendering them near-invisible to the aliens' sensors, and blurring them visually.

Squad Nine didn't have a nickname like Hell Squad. But with Roth and Theron as the only two men, a few people had tried to give them some pretty lame ones. Roth smiled to himself. Once, someone at one of the base's Friday night parties, after too many homebrews, had called Squad Nine the Harem.

The women, some of the best soldiers he'd ever served with, had taken offense. After that, no one had ever dared to mention the word harem again. No one had even dared give them another nickname. His smile widened. His squad was tough, a little mean when riled, and it was best not to cross them.

They reminded him of his little sister, Gwen. She would have been exactly like the women on his team. His smile dissolved away. If she'd ever had the chance to grow into a woman.

Roth's gut tightened, and he forced the ghosts of past failures away. His only focus now was on fighting the aliens. He had to be better, faster and smarter. He had to make sure no one on his team got hurt.

An explosion of shouts from Hell Squad knocked Roth out of his thoughts.

"Fuck me. What the hell is that?"

Roth recognized the voice of Hell Squad's sniper, Shaw. Roth peered out the cockpit windscreen, but the Darkswift had moved too far around. He tapped the controls. "Turning back. Anyone got a visual?" he asked his team.

As the glider turned in a sharp but graceful arc, he heard an indrawn breath through his earpiece.

"Boss, I can see it." It was Taylor. The brunette was the best shot on his team, and had eyesight like a bird. "It's some sort of...crocodile-like alien. Not sure how to describe it, but it can *move*. It's attacking Hell Squad."

Finally, the Darkswift leveled out, and Roth got a good look down below. "Hell."

The alien did look like a crocodile, but not like any living today. This sucker had long legs, and was galloping toward the squad, leaving a trail of water from the harbor. The damn thing had been lying in wait.

Hell Squad opened fire with their laser carbines, concentrating their blasts on the creature. It had tough, dark skin and long, snapping jaws filled with sharp teeth. It also had those demonic, red glowing eyes all the aliens possessed.

And dammit, the laser fire wasn't making much of a dent in the animal's heavy, protective scales.

"Hell Squad, get out of range. Squad Nine, aim your fire on the creature." Roth glanced at his second. "Mac?"

"Got it." She thumbed the controls, lining up the Darkswift's laser cannon to aim at the giant alien creature. Her brow was creased in concentration.

A second later, laser fire spewed from the three Darkswifts, lighting up the afternoon air with traces of green.

This time, the creature stopped. It spun in an ungainly circle and then raced back toward the water.

"Keep firing," Roth yelled. "Take it down."

But the creature appeared impervious to the laser cannon. It ran at full speed back toward the harbor, looking more like some giant dog than a crocodile. Then it leapt into the water with a huge splash.

The Darkswifts ceased fire. Roth circled over the water, but soon all he could see were tiny ripples in the near-smooth surface. No sign of the alien.

"Roth," the calm, competent voice of Squad Nine's comms officer, Arden, came through the line. "A raptor patrol just appeared on the screen. Five hundred meters to the east."

Each squad had comms officers back at base, who fed them intel gathered by small drones. Arden was quiet, competent and dependable. When she spoke, they listened. Roth muttered a curse. He'd known the aliens' absence had been temporary, but they'd hoped it would last longer than this. "Steele—"

"We see them, Masters. Engaging."

Roth flew overhead, ready to offer assistance.

It wasn't necessary.

Roth watched Hell Squad do what they did best. They mowed through the humanoid alien raptors like some sort of living machine, even though the bastards were all over six and half feet tall and made of pure muscle. He listened to Shaw and the others yell and make smart-ass comments. Roth shook his head. If he didn't know better, he'd say that Hell Squad had missed fighting the aliens.

"Raptors are down," Marcus said. "Thanks for your help, Nine."

"You got it, Marcus." Roth nodded at Mac. "Heading back to base. Hell Squad, a Hawk is en route to pick you up." Even as Roth said the words, he saw the dark shape of the quadcopter appear in the sky as it dropped its illusion. Its four rotors were spinning and it was descending right to Hell Squad's location.

Once he knew that Marcus' team was taken care of, Roth turned his craft to head west. "Okay, Nine," he said. "Let's head back to base."

Almost as one, the three Darkswifts wheeled around and fell into formation, one on each side of Roth's craft. With their destination locked in, and the ground beneath just a blur, Roth's thoughts turned dark. Today's encounter confirmed that the aliens were heading back into the streets. They'd be rounding up more and more human survivors to take back to their ship, to shove into alien tanks and to strap down in labs to experiment on.

He let out a long breath. This battle with the aliens continued to feel like they were taking one step forward, followed by three steps back. Humans needed more intel; they needed an edge, something bigger. Something much more damaging. They were never going to be able to defeat the aliens and survive as a species if they just kept annoying the aliens like a swarm of insects.

They had to hurt them.

Santha Kade's team of recon officers was doing a great job of sneaking into alien territory, gathering intel, and getting back out. They were working on the problem, trying to find something—anything—that might help tip the balance and finally let them win this damn war. It just wasn't happening fast enough for Roth.

He knew better than anyone that you couldn't get complacent. His chest constricted. You had to push forward, you had to take the offensive. If you just waited around, people died.

He also suspected there was someone on base who knew more—much more—about the aliens than she was sharing. And he didn't like that one bit.

"What's put that mean look on your face?"

He didn't look at Mac. As his second-in-command, she'd gotten damn good at reading him, and it was annoying as hell. "Nothing."

Mac snorted. "Liar."

Yeah, he was. Because he was thinking about a woman he'd pulled out of one of those damn alien tanks. A woman who'd fought him with a skilled fierceness he reluctantly admired.

A woman who could give him exactly what he needed—he just had to put more pressure on her until she cracked.

***

Avery juggled the heavy box in her arms and tossed

the last few vegetables in.

"Hey, careful with those," snapped a voice.

She turned and hid a grin. "Quit bitching, old man. I won't hurt your precious carrots."

Old Man Hamish—all weathered, wrinkled skin and spiky gray hair—huffed out a breath, but she could tell he was trying not to smile. Everyone else tiptoed around the man who kept Blue Mountain Base's hydroponic garden blooming and well-stocked, but Avery didn't. She knew that under the cranky bluster he was just lonely. She'd had a lifetime of experience spotting lonely.

"You are a mouthy one," Hamish grumbled, plucking at his checked shirt.

"And you love it." She cocked her hip. "Why worry about the carrots and potatoes? They're just going to get chopped up and tossed in a pot."

"Because I want them to taste good. People in this rabbit warren deserve something nice."

Avery's smile melted away. That was the truth. "I'll take good care of them. Like I always do." She'd been reduced to agent in charge of vegetables. It was a far cry from her job as a special agent for the Coalition Central Intelligence Agency.

Forcing the frustration away, she turned her attention back to the box.

Hamish's cloudy blue eyes narrowed. "Still got you slaving away in the kitchens?"

"We all have to help out."

"You should do what you're good at," the old man said. "I'm pretty sure that ain't chopping and stirring."

A heavy knot tied up her insides. Once, she'd prided herself on being good at her job. At protecting people, and defeating the bad guys.

Then she'd failed, and that failure had killed billions of people.

"The medical team won't give me clearance." She'd been among those rescued from an alien lab. And even though she'd been lucky and hadn't suffered any injuries, the doctors were being cautious. It grated. Avery wanted to be out there fighting, not in here cooking. "And anyway, I'm not sure what I'm good at anymore, Hamish." Avery hefted the box higher, not sure where those words had come from. "Besides, I enjoy coming down here and trading barbs with you too much."

Hamish crossed his arms and scowled. "You'd do better on the squads, going out there and fighting those damn aliens."

That knot got tighter. "Thanks for the vegetables, Hamish. See you later." She pushed open the door with her hip and escaped.

As she made her way down the tunnel, her shoes echoed softly on the concrete. She tried not to think about the past, but it slammed into her like a hard punch to the gut.

Well, some of it did. There were a lot of blank patches and blurry memories she couldn't make out, no matter how hard she tried. Out of the ones she could recall, there were some memories she wasn't certain were real or imagined.

At the junction of three tunnels, she turned left, heading for the ramp up to the kitchens and main living quarters. After living here in Blue Mountain Base for the past several weeks, she knew her way around. It was home to hundreds, a haven from the alien apocalypse above.

An apocalypse she'd been tasked with preventing. *Yeah, you did a brilliant job there, Avery.*

A headache sprung up behind her right eye and she gripped the cardboard box tighter.

She'd been the golden child at the Coalition Central Intelligence Agency. Special Agent Stillman had been on the rise, bringing down bad guys, fighting terrorists, protecting the Coalition's citizens.

Her headache spiked up a notch and she hoofed it up the ramp. She remembered when the aliens, the Gizzida, had made contact with the Coalition. She remembered the initial negotiation meetings...then nothing. Nothing until she'd been yanked from a tank in the alien's huge Genesis Facility by the base's squads. She'd woken, disoriented, with huge holes poked in her memories.

And no matter how hard she tried, she couldn't remember where she'd been the last year.

Frustration grew inside of her, and Avery powered down the corridor more quickly, turning a corner and nearly mowing down someone. "Oh...sorry."

"No problem." Elle Milton smiled at Avery. "It's Avery, right?"

"Yes." Avery knew she shouldn't be wary of the

pretty, dark-haired woman. But she knew that Elle was the comms officer for Hell Squad. Avery lifted the box an inch. "I need to get these to the kitchen."

As she started back down the corridor, Elle settled into step beside her. Avery swallowed a groan.

"I'm heading to the landing pads. Squad Six is on their way back."

Squad Six was Hell Squad's official name. Avery just nodded.

"And Squad Nine. They were out on recon." The woman wrinkled her nose. "Came across a new kind of alien."

Oh, Avery wanted to pepper Elle with questions, but she wasn't an agent anymore...she was just a kitchen hand with a memory like Swiss cheese. Instead, she bit her tongue and made an appropriate noise.

"How are you settling in?" Elle asked.

"Fine." Avery winced. Oh, that didn't sound terse or defensive at all.

The other woman just smiled. "I don't see you around much."

"Chef keeps me pretty busy in the kitchens." *And I spend the rest of my time in my quarters, either trying to remember, or working out to regain my fitness.*

A bright smile lit up the woman's face. "The man is a genius. Crazy that aliens can invade, and we can all still eat well." Her gaze traced over Avery's. "If you need to get out, or need someone to talk to, I'm always available."

Right. When she wasn't shacked up with one of the most dangerous men in the base—Hell Squad's leader, Marcus Steele. Avery just couldn't work out how the pretty former socialite and the rough, scarred soldier went together. But Elle had an almost incandescent look on her face. One that screamed happiness, even in the middle of hell.

Avery felt a sharp stab of...something. She shook her head. It was crazy to care for someone when the world had gone to hell. Especially someone who went out there every day to wade through it. As far as Avery could see, Elle's happiness was on shaky ground. "Thanks. I do need to get back."

Elle's smile dimmed a little. "Sure thing. Bye."

Avery quickened her steps. The door into the kitchen appeared ahead. Elle seemed nice, but Avery just couldn't seem to make herself befriend people. Part of that was learned from her time being shuffled around the foster care system. You befriended people and cared about them at your own risk. The next day, someone would be there to take you away, and your new "friend" would be gone.

The other part of her wanted to scream at everyone—*I'm the one responsible for all of this. You living deep underground, dressed in second-hand clothes and all your loved ones dead, because of me.*

She wasn't sure she could be free and easy, like Elle. And she was damn certain she'd never radiate happiness.

Avery reached the door, jammed the box between the wall and her hip, then slapped a hand to the door lock. She quickly grabbed the box again and as the lock beeped, she pushed through the door.

Delicious scents assailed her. She had to admit, the food in the base was good. Definitely much better than the frozen dinners she'd lived on before. Since she'd been pulled from that alien tank—and thank the lord, she hadn't been in there long enough to start the transformation from human to alien—she'd quickly gotten used to eating well here at Blue Mountain.

The man in charge, General Adam Holmes, ran the base with smooth precision, and she couldn't fault the work he'd done. He'd worked hard to transform the former military base into a home—with living quarters, a school, an infirmary, and dozens of storage rooms for any and all scavenged goods they could find. Still, at the end of the day, it was a military base as well, home to those squads who went out to fight the aliens every single day.

"Took your time, Av."

Avery set the box on a shiny silver workbench and looked up at the enormous man nearby.

The massive giant of a man didn't seem to have a name, going simply by Chef. He was six foot eight with massive shoulders, skin the color of black coffee, and most often a wide, easy smile. He was the friendliest man she'd ever met...unless you messed up any of his food.

Then he could be downright cranky.

"Keep your hat on, Chef. I had to work my charm on Old Man Hamish. You know he begrudges every floret of broccoli that leaves his gardens."

Chef made a harrumphing sound. "Bring it over here. I need to get that spinach in the stew."

She set down the vegetables he'd asked for. "Heaven forbid we don't have enough spinach in your masterpiece."

"No respect," Chef muttered, but his teeth flashed white in his face.

She shook her head, smiling. "Temperamental."

"Don't know why I put up with you."

Avery started unpacking the rest of the vegetables. She knew they were lucky to have the fresh stuff at all. The shelves behind her were stacked with cans and dry goods that had been scavenged over the year and a half since the invasion, but slowly those stocks were dwindling, and eventually, they would run out. "You put up with me, Chef, because no one else will work with you."

"We both know you won't stay working in here for long."

Her hand paused, clutching a leek. She deliberately placed it on the chopping board. "Trying to get rid of me already?"

"Nope. But, girl, you have skills...they'll decide to use them."

Avery closed her eyes. First Hamish, now Chef. She should have kept her mouth shut about her past employment. It was true, she wanted to be out there, fighting, helping bring these aliens down, but for now, she was grounded. "I have some pretty mad kitchen skills, too. You need them."

Chef snorted. "Girl, you can barely boil water. That's why I make you chop and stir."

She shot him a smile...just as the kitchen door slammed open. She turned and froze. *Not again.*

Roth Masters strode in, still wearing his lower body armor. On top he wore a simple, faded, green T-shirt that stretched across a broad chest and shoulders. The neckline was soaked with sweat and his dog tags hung in the center of his hard chest. His rugged face was set in hard lines, his sandy hair falling over his forehead, and his ice-blue eyes were laser-focused.

On her.

Chapter Two

Avery stiffened. The leader of Squad Nine was over six feet of alpha male. He oozed his take-charge, in-control attitude like pheromones.

Cranky, stubborn, alpha-male pheromones. At least, they were to her. She eyed the corded muscles in his biceps, and the hint of the ridges his T-shirt clung to, her gaze drawn there against her will. She'd always been attracted to raw strength and power. How could such an annoying man come in such a delectable package?

He paused near her. "Agent Stillman."

Avery ground her teeth together and resumed unpacking her box. "Masters, I've told you, just Avery will do."

"I need you to come with me."

He had a smooth, deep voice for such a muscular, rugged man. If she closed her eyes, that voice conjured up the image of a handsome man in a tailored suit.

"Now," he continued.

Her chest went tight. "We're going to do this dance again? For the third time this week?" She spun and faced him, her hands on her hips. "Me and you across a table, you battering me with questions I can't answer."

"Won't answer."

"I don't remember!" She slapped a hand against the bench, and ignored the sting to her palm. "Why can't I get that through your thick head?"

He took a step closer, crowding her close. "Because I saw the records on that damn alien ship. You starred in all of them. You met with those fuckers before the invasion. You negotiated with them."

Avery heaved in a breath. That negotiation was something she'd clearly sucked at. She just loved having Roth Masters rub her face in it. And on top of that, he was a big fat reminder that he got to go out there and fight, and she didn't. Anger stormed through her blood. She leaned in, until they were barely an inch apart. "And for my trouble, I got shoved in an alien genesis tank, remember?"

His hand shot out and gripped her arm.

She ignored the zing she felt where his fingers touched her skin. Instead, she let her training take over. She chopped a hand to his arm, saw him flinch, and broke his hold. *I could take you, Masters, if I really wanted.*

A muscle ticked in his jaw. He grabbed her other arm, fingers biting into her skin.

"I don't remember anything, Masters." Except fear, and pain—horrible pain. Her mouth flooding with fluid, and burning through her body. No, she wasn't going there. She straightened her spine. "I don't remember."

His fingers tightened on her arm, but he was silent, watching her.

She lifted her chin. "My clearest memory is you. Pulling me from that tank."

Those eyes like chips of ice. She remembered those in glorious detail.

He'd been the one who'd pulled her out of the tank. He'd stopped her hurting herself or anyone else. He'd held her with those strong arms. And she saw those pale-blue eyes in her dreams.

Stupid. She also remembered that in her disorientation, she'd attacked him. In the scuffle, she'd given him a black eye, while he'd been careful not to hurt her.

"Girl's been through enough, Masters," Chef said, his voice rumbling with displeasure.

Masters was still staring at her. Then his jaw firmed. He tugged her away from the bench. "We all have. I need answers."

Avery sighed. "Fine. Let's dance."

***

Roth turned and put his hands on his hips. Special Agent Stillman sat at the battered metal table in the interrogation room, her face composed. They'd been at it for an hour, and he'd gotten nothing.

She looked tired. There were dark circles under her eyes. When she caught him staring, she lifted her chin, her eyes sparking.

She had spirit, that was for sure. She'd looked the same way when she'd come out of the tank—

wet and bedraggled, but fighting. He turned away, looking at the one-way mirror back into the corridor. He knew his good friend, Captain Laura Bladon, head of the interrogation team and the prison cells, was out there, observing.

He turned back. "Okay, so you say you can't remember anything about the invasion or how you ended up in the Genesis Facility."

Avery huffed out a breath. "Yes. I've mentioned that, about a hundred times."

"What's your last clear memory? What do you remember?"

A crease appeared on her brow and she tapped one long finger on the table. "I believe it was the first meeting we had with the Gizzida."

"So they made contact and asked for a meet?"

She nodded. "They contacted the Coalition leaders, told us they were here in our solar system. We suspected they may have contacted other world leaders, as well. But they swore us to secrecy, so it was never confirmed."

"How did they communicate?"

"They had someone translating." She rubbed her temple.

"Okay. Where did you meet them?"

"The meeting was arranged in the central Australian desert. We didn't want to alarm anyone, so they flew down in a smaller ship to the meet."

"And then what happened?"

"Their ship...it was larger than the ptero ships they use down here, but not as large as that monstrosity they invaded Sydney in."

Roth nodded. It made sense they'd have something in between. "Go on."

"It looked like some giant kind of insect." She rubbed her temple again, her frown deepening. "After it landed, a group of raptors emerged. All large humanoids, with thick skin, reptilian-like features."

"And the translator?"

"He—I think it was a he—was a raptor. He had a very heavy accent, but he spoke English." She stared off at the wall. "He seemed smaller than the others."

Roth grunted. His tablet lay on the table, lights blinking as it recorded their conversation. "What did they ask for?"

Now she was rubbing her temple vigorously. "They told us they came from the...some system. What we call the Alphard system. They...they said they had an armada of ships waiting on the other side of the moon. They could wipe us out." She winced now. "Uh...I think they...damn headache."

"What did they want, Stillman?"

"I..." Hazel eyes, an intriguing blend of green and gold, looked up at him. "I don't know. I can't remember."

Dammit. "You *need* to remember. The survival of the human race could depend on it."

She shoved to her feet. "Don't you think I know that?"

He couldn't tear his gaze off her face. She always looked defiant to him, but right now he saw a flash of something else—pain? Vulnerability?

"You might be the perfect soldier and never make a mistake. But the rest of us mortals can't say the same."

Roth felt a muscle tick in his jaw. He was far from perfect. "I'm just a soldier."

"I know you were part of the Special Operations Command." There was a slight sneer on her face. "An elite group, the best of the best. Even though everyone knew SOC was just the military's assassins."

Roth released a breath. "This isn't about me. It's about what you know about the aliens."

Avery pressed her hands to her head. "You think I'm not trying to remember? I go to bed every night knowing I did something wrong and billions died. Something I can't damn well remember. I toss and turn every night trying to get my head—" she thumped it with her palm "—to release something, anything that might help."

Sympathy charged through him. Jesus, maybe he'd pushed her too hard. "Stillman—"

"You know what, screw you, Masters." She wrapped her arms around herself.

There was a hard knock at the door, then it opened. Captain Laura Bladon stepped inside. Her red hair was pulled back in a ponytail and her face was set in hard lines. "Enough." She jerked her head at the door.

Roth watched Avery round the table and drop into the chair. With a sigh, he followed Laura out.

"You're pushing her a bit hard, aren't you?" the former Navy Intelligence Officer said.

Roth pressed his hands to the edge of the one-way mirror and watched Avery. Hell, who was he kidding, he couldn't take his eyes off her. A part of him wanted to go in there and pull her into his arms. Comfort her.

Frowning, he wondered who she'd been spending time with. She'd come out of the alien lab uninjured, unlike so many others who were still recovering from terrible experimentation, but she was obviously suffering some aftereffects. Dammit, maybe she really didn't remember.

"She's the key, Laura. She knows something that can help us beat these aliens, I know it."

"This is the third time you've had her in here this week. Push too hard and she might break. Then you'll get nothing."

So far, all he thought Avery wanted to do was knee him in the balls, or gut him with something dull and rusty. But Laura was in charge of the base's prison and interrogation team because she was good. She knew what she was talking about.

He raked a hand through his hair and looked again at Avery. He was pushing her too hard, and he knew, deep down, it wasn't just about her. It was about his own dark secrets, his own guilt.

She lifted her head, staring at the mirror like she knew he was there. Stubborn fire burned in her eyes. He didn't think she'd break. She was too damn tough for that.

"Let her go," he told Laura. Then he turned and walked away.

***

Avery tucked the small scraps of leftovers from the night's meal into her pocket. Out in the base's dining room, she could still hear the murmur of voices and the tinkle of cutlery on plates.

"I'm out of here, Chef," she called.

"Righty-o, Av. Have a good one."

She waved and slipped into the tunnel. The corridor was empty and she hurried in the direction of the western exit. It was the perfect time, with everyone still busy with dinner.

She passed close to the Hawk hangers and heard people talking. Probably the quadcopter mechanics carrying out maintenance. The small fleet of Hawks were vital for getting the squads in and out on their missions. They'd apparently lost one, just before Avery had come to the base—and they'd almost lost Hell Squad in the crash, too. So they were extra careful with the remaining ones. She itched to be in there, her hand running over smooth metal, preparing for a mission.

Hunching her shoulders, she turned a corner and headed for the ladder to the surface. She climbed up quickly, bypassed the security on the hatch at the top and climbed out.

Avery stood for a second and simply breathed in the brisk night air. It wasn't cold. Summer was coming, and she could smell it in the spring-laden breeze and the promise of warmth. Still, up here in the mountains, the nights stayed cooler.

She hurried into the trees, and wondered if he'd

be waiting for her.

She reached a fallen log and sat down. Gum trees towered above her and through the leaves, she could see the stars. They made her stomach tighten. Before the Gizzida, she'd looked at the stars in wonder, now she looked in dread. It made her wonder how many other warlike, advanced species were out there with their gazes turned toward Earth.

Chafing her arms with her hands, she forced her thoughts away from aliens. Masters had peppered her with questions on them enough for today. She chewed her lip. Not that she really blamed him. He was a man dedicated to protecting others. He wanted to help. Hell, she'd been exactly like that in her job. Before.

"Dino?" she called out quietly. "You there?"

All she heard was the buzzing of insects and something rustling high in the trees. Probably a possum. She tapped her fingers against her thigh. It wasn't like him to be late.

"Special Agent Stillman, you know civilians aren't permitted out of the base at night, or alone."

With an internal groan, Avery turned. "Every damn time I turn around..."

Roth crossed his arms. He was wearing jeans and a white T-shirt that was stretched dangerously tight over all his muscles. Couldn't the guy find a bigger size? She knew the clothing store at the base was a bit limited for choice, but still.

"I'm not planning anything devious. I just needed some air."

"How did you get out without setting off the alarms?"

"Special agent, remember?" She could hack a military-grade encryption if she had to. She hadn't forgotten everything.

He glanced around. "I heard you calling for someone."

She rolled her eyes. "Right. I'm planning a secret military coup with the aliens. My contact should be here any second."

His blue eyes narrowed. She felt so incredibly irritated that the 'annoyed and suspicious' look made his face look sexy.

Suddenly, there was the patter of footsteps and a small dog leapt out of the trees and landed on the log beside her.

Roth relaxed. "A dog."

"Yep. Masters, meet Dino. Dino, this is Mr. Stubborn Masters."

The dog shoved his wet nose into her shirt, searching for the food scraps. She laughed and patted his matted brown fur.

Masters stepped closer. "He looks like a mutt."

"Definitely. I think he has a bit of everything in him." She gave Dino the scraps and he scarfed them down. She smiled. "No manners."

"Dino?"

She shrugged. "Seemed appropriate, considering."

Masters moved until he could stroke the dog. "Needs a bath."

"I tried to brush him once. He wasn't a fan."

Masters leaned against a nearby tree. She felt his gaze on her like a physical thing. "Did you have a dog as a kid?"

"Hell, no." When he raised an eyebrow, she shrugged. "I was in the system. Unless a foster home had a dog, I couldn't have a pet." She couldn't have anything. She felt him scrutinizing her and shifted on the log. "Did you just follow me out here to catch me doing something I shouldn't be doing? Or did you want to interrogate me some more?"

"I spotted you sneaking out—"

She jumped to her feet and faced him. "I wasn't sneaking!" Okay, maybe she'd been sneaking a little. "Well, not much. I just needed some time alone."

"Do you...have any friends at base?"

She blinked. What the hell did that have to do with anything? "None of your goddamned business, Masters. I am not some alien spy, I am not withholding information—"

The dog's gaze settled on Roth and he growled. They both ignored him.

Avery stepped closer, her boots bumping Masters'. "How the hell do I convince you I'm not holding back?"

"Dammit." He shoved a hand through his hair. "I'm just trying to do what's right."

"I get that, but can you stop riding me so hard? You keep it up, and I'll have carpet burn."

As soon as the words came out, the air between them changed. Took on a charged quality. Avery felt her eyes widen, and her heart start thumping hard in her chest. She hadn't meant it to sound so…sexual.

They stared at each other. She could smell him—soap and man—and felt the warmth pouring off him. To her horror, she felt her nipples pucker.

She took a step back, snapping the spell. Roth Masters was a pain in her butt—and dammit, even that sounded wrong. He was an annoyance, nothing else.

"Just stay out of my way, Masters, and I'll stay out of yours." She patted the dog one last time, then turned and tried to tell herself she wasn't beating a retreat.

Chapter Three

The base's regular Friday night gathering was in full swing. Roth sipped his homebrewed beer and leaned back in his chair. He was waiting for the annoying tension in his shoulders to ease. So far, neither the homebrew, nor the conversation with his squad was helping.

A few people were playing instruments off to the side. No one had quite the magical touch of Hell Squad's second-in-command, Cruz Ramos, but his partner Santha was pregnant and apparently suffering morning sickness...and not just in the morning. So Roth didn't expect to see the man out partying.

"Ugh, I would kill for a nice, crisp chardonnay." Taylor plopped down beside him.

With the face of a beauty queen and dark hair that glinted red in the light, people often made the mistake of thinking she wasn't a hell of a soldier. Big mistake.

She wrinkled her nose. "This homebrew sucks."

"It's not that bad," he said. "But it's not chardonnay."

Taylor took a long swig from her bottle. "No. It's not."

Mac leaned forward from Roth's other side. "Looks like the aliens are getting pretty busy again out on the streets. I'd really hoped you and Hell Squad damaging their energy source would have put them down for longer."

Roth had hoped so too. "With the energy cubes we destroyed, it'll take time for them to replace them, at least. It'll also take time for them to make more of those genesis tanks."

"Thank God for small favors." A tall woman sauntered up. Camryn McNab had gorgeous dark skin she'd inherited from her African mother, and a Scottish burr she'd picked up from her Highlander father. She leaned against the table. Unless she was in the field, Cam didn't stand if she could sit. Hell, she'd lie down, if she could.

He watched two nearby men with their gazes glued to Cam. The rest of the squad called her the glamazon. She liked to dress up when she wasn't in fatigues or armor. Right now, she had on some tight, black pants and a tiny halter top that showed off her toned shoulders. Roth always pictured her as an ancient queen lounging on cushions while being carried around on a litter. But put a carbine in her hands and she turned into a warrior.

The final two members of his squad arrived. Sienna Rossi—all long, dark curls and a curvy body—was talking a mile a minute to the tall, silent Theron. Roth nodded to them both. Theron didn't say much, but he didn't seem to mind being surrounded by tough, deadly females. He was a quiet man by nature, but a bull in a firefight.

Roth sipped his beer and fell back into brooding. These gatherings helped everyone blow off steam, which was vitally important when the world had gone to hell. Even more important when people had lost their loved ones, and needed a sense of closeness. For many, the night ended up in someone's bed. Casual sex wasn't frowned upon here. Since the invasion, it was embraced as a way to feel close to someone else. He'd taken up the odd offer, but for the most part, he spent the majority of his time with the squads, and the rest of the time planning future missions.

"What's up with the boss?" Cam drawled. "All this broody silence isn't his style."

Roth ignored Cam's comment. He'd gotten used to ignoring them when they started poking at him.

"Not sure," Mac answered, talking over him like he wasn't even there. "He was questioning that CCIA agent again. After that, he was cranky as hell. So I guess he didn't get what he wanted."

"Hmm." Cam dragged the sound out in a way that set Roth on edge. "And just what did he want, I wonder?"

Roth took another deliberate sip of his beer and kept ignoring them.

Across the room, he caught Marcus Steele's green gaze, and the head of Hell Squad nodded. The man had his arm around Elle Milton. Talk about beauty and the beast. The battle-hardened soldier and the former socialite, but strangely, the two of them fit. When Elle looked up and said something to Marcus, the big man smiled.

Happiness and love. Roth took another swig of beer to ease his suddenly tight throat. Even in the middle of a war, these two had found it.

Beside them stood the rest of Hell Squad, minus Cruz and Santha. Gabe Jackson—in Roth's opinion Hell Squad's deadliest soldier—stood tall and silent. Beside him a blonde woman gesticulated enthusiastically as she told some story. Dr. Emerson Green was a hell of a doctor who ran the base's medical team. She'd patched Roth up more times than he could count, and the rest of his team as well. He watched her laugh, then elbow Gabe. The man managed a small smile—and that was a minor miracle. Roth wondered if anyone else saw the all-consuming love in Gabe's eyes.

Hell Squad's explosives expert, Reed, stood with his arms around a dark-haired woman. Natalya had survived horrible experimentation by the aliens, but here she was, smiling, snuggling into Reed.

Roth remembered his mother cuddling his father. He'd had a house full of love growing up. His mother had been a teacher, his father a laser ball coach. They'd adored their children, and demonstrated that fact regularly. Roth and Gwen had been raised in a house full of learning, love and laughter.

Until everything had been torn apart and Roth's life had changed in an instant.

After joining the Army, and later the special team at the Special Operations Command—an elite group of soldiers from all branches of the military—

Roth hadn't thought much about love. All he'd wanted was to serve his country. To protect others, to make sure the innocent didn't die.

And since the alien attack, well, hell, there wasn't any damn time to think about love.

But since the members of Hell Squad kept falling in love, it was kind of in his face all the time. He caught two ladies nearby, trying to snag his attention. They smiled, lifting their drinks to him. He nodded. He didn't know the curvy brunette, but the tall, luscious blonde was named Liberty. She took care of the base's clothing store, and apparently ran a successful underground market in beauty products. He was aware that many people dismissed the importance of having those items, but he suspected Liberty knew. Having clothes and looking good, recreating some small semblance of life before the aliens, helped people cope.

He'd also heard she was a wild ride in bed, and open about her enjoyment of sex with a hard-bodied man. He looked away. There were plenty of single ladies in the base who came here to snag a soldier for the night. They were honest, upfront, and kept it easy.

Shit. Why wasn't that more appealing? He tapped a finger against his beer bottle. He didn't have much time for sex, and to be honest, the inclination just wasn't there most of the time. Maybe he was too focused, too driven.

He let his gaze drift over the room, and it zeroed in on a dark head.

Everything in him roared to life.

Apparently, the inclination was back.

Avery was pushing through the crowd, trying not to spill some bubbly, orange drink. The big bulk of Chef was beside her, along with the chef's boyfriend, Danny, a slender man who worked on the tech team.

Roth's hand clenched on his bottle. *Dammit.* He needed answers from her, not a roll in his bunk. Instantly, the image of Avery laid out on his bed made him go hard. He shook his head. Hell, she wouldn't be laid out, she'd be giving as good as she got, probably wrestling him for the top. Sinking those white teeth into his skin.

He'd not seen her at one of these gatherings before. As she, Chef and Danny found a place to stand, Roth noticed the nearby men in the room taking notice of her.

She wasn't dressed up like some of the other women, but she still stood out. Her dark hair was loose for a change, brushing her shoulders, and her face was strong—high cheekbones, bold nose, a full mouth.

But it was the way she moved that made her memorable. She might not remember everything from before, but she moved with a confidence that drew people to notice her.

"Earth to Masters? Masters?"

Roth blinked and saw Mac waving a hand in front of his face. "What?"

"God, you are crabby today." She dangled a bottle in front of his face. "Do you want another drink? Or you want to ogle the CCIA agent some more?"

God, sometimes he wished for a squad of men who wouldn't poke and prod at him over personal stuff. He released a breath. Another beer might help dull this edginess running through him, but he suspected only one thing would really help him. "No."

Mac raised a brow. "To the beer or the ogling?"

He stood and scowled at her. "The beer, Carides."

He stalked through the crowd. Chef and Danny had gone to the bar and Avery was sipping her drink and studying the room.

He stopped right behind her. "Agent Stillman."

Her head whipped around. "Jesus, you just won't leave me alone, will you?"

He dragged in a deep breath. "I'm not here to question you."

She snorted. "Not this time."

"I believe...that you can't remember everything."

Her eyes widened. "Wow, a small miracle just occurred."

He took the empty space beside her, unprepared for when his shoulder brushed hers, scattering his thoughts for a second. "I'm sorry. I've been fighting these aliens for over a year, I've seen what they've done... I need to do whatever the hell I have to do to beat them. I know I can get a bit..."

"Overbearing? Domineering?"

He felt his jaw harden.

She blew out a breath. "Look, I get it."

"You do?"

She fiddled with her drink, running one finger around the rim of the glass. "Yeah. Working out how to beat the bad guys...that used to be my job."

Roth suspected she had a lot of hidden talents. Talents that were wasted peeling potatoes. "Why not join the squads?"

Something flashed over her face before the shutters came down. "Because who knows when and where these damn blanks in my head will appear." She looked at him, her hazel eyes catching his. "Medical refuses to clear me. Besides, I'm a security risk, right?" She straightened and set her drink down. "Enough people have died because of my incompetence." She bit her lip, then spun and hurried out of the room.

Roth closed his eyes. God, he'd messed that up.

Chef appeared, his hands filled with drinks. "Dammit, Masters. Can't you just leave her alone?"

Roth stared at the empty doorway. No, it seemed he couldn't do that.

***

Avery wasn't sure why she'd come into the empty dining room. She just knew she didn't want to be back in her tiny quarters.

The lights were off, the long tables empty. Just a light from the kitchen cast a faint glow in the room. She started pacing.

God, she hated feeling so useless like this. She rested against the edge of a table and pressed her head into her hands. She was so tired of feeling like a failure. Tears pricked her eyes and she sniffed. She never cried. At the agency, they'd called her Tough-as-Nails Stillman. She'd battled madmen, talked down the criminally insane, and interrogated terrorists, all without flinching.

"I'm sorry."

Roth's voice made her jerk. She swiped a hand at her eyes. She hadn't heard him at all. For a big man he moved very quietly.

"Can't you just leave me alone?" she said.

"Apparently, I can't." He moved out of the shadows, a big, strong silhouette.

She spun to face him, all the feelings of pain, anger, guilt, and uselessness coalescing inside her. She slammed her palms against his chest. "I can't give you the answers you want. I would if I could."

He grabbed her hands, his large ones engulfing hers. Avery was tall for a woman, and she was used to being strong. She wasn't used to feeling smaller or weaker than anyone else.

His fingers rubbed at her wrists, her forearms. "Jesus, you're wound so tight."

She tried to pull away from him, but he held fast. "I'm not your concern."

"You really stay awake at night trying to remember?"

"Yes. I've tried every technique I know to stimulate my memories. I know there's a chance that I know things that could help against the aliens." Why was she talking to him? She put some more strength into her struggle to get her hands free. "Let me go."

"No."

Anger spiked. "Fine." She brought her knee up, fast and hard. She hit his thigh and heard him grunt, but he didn't retaliate.

She kicked at his knee, but standing this close to him, she couldn't get a lot of power behind it. Next, she rammed their joined hands up, aiming for his nose.

But he was ready, and faster than she'd guessed. He stopped her hands, shifting closer to crowd her.

Avery swung to the side and this time aimed her knee at his crotch.

"Dammit." He let her go.

But Avery wasn't thinking anymore. She just wanted to lash out, to hurt. She spun and slammed a hard side kick into his gut.

He cursed and she gritted her teeth. Damn, the man was all muscle. She kept attacking, throwing punches, hits and kicks.

Meanwhile, he was doing everything he could to block her without hurting her.

"Dammit, Stillman."

She slammed her foot into his side and he staggered a little. "Call me Avery, damn you." She jumped, aiming her roundhouse kick for his head.

Roth charged forward, grabbed her around the middle and lifted her off her feet.

Next thing she knew, she was flat on her back on the nearest table, Roth's big body covering hers.

"Calm down...Avery."

Her chest was heaving against his hard one. "Was that so difficult?"

"No." One of his hands was planted beside her face. He moved it, his palm touching her cheek. "You are damn good with hand-to-hand."

"I barely touched you."

"I don't think you were actually trying to hurt me."

"That's what you think," she muttered.

"Avery, you need to talk to someone. You're holding everything that happened to you inside. If you keep it bottled up, it'll take you down."

"Why do you care?" She looked at the wall.

His other hand cupped the other side of her face and forced her to look at him. His rugged face was only an inch away from hers.

"I care."

A shiver snaked through her, warmth curling low down in her belly.

"Avery..."

She felt herself softening, her body leaning into his. No. She couldn't do this. She needed the antagonism to keep him at bay. She didn't need the understanding she saw shimmering in his eyes. She didn't need anyone, didn't want anyone else close enough, because she knew how easy it was for people to walk away.

"Damn you," she said shakily.

She grabbed his stubbled cheeks and yanked his mouth to hers.

Roth stiffened, then he groaned. His lips took over, his mouth moving against hers.

He tasted good. Really good. Avery bit his bottom lip, and then his tongue was slipping into her mouth. He tilted her head, taking the kiss deeper.

The pleasure was pulling her under. It would be so easy to lose herself in it, to learn to crave it.

She yanked her mouth away and pushed against his chest. "Off."

His weight lifted and Avery scrambled off the table. For a second, she felt lightheaded and unsteady on her feet.

She looked at Roth, and was gratified to see he looked as shell-shocked as she did.

She scraped a hand through her messed-up hair. She felt just like her hair must look. Messed up, her mind like a sponge full of holes. She didn't need the very large, and sure to be very demanding, complication standing in front of her.

He was a risk she just wasn't prepared to take.

"I'll try to remember what I can," she said, taking a step toward the door.

"Avery—"

"If I remember anything, I'll let you know." And for the second time that night—or was it the third?—Avery hotfooted it away from Roth Masters.

Chapter Four

"All right, everyone. Let's try breaking those reverse holds again. Turn to your partner." Roth, hands on his hips, stalked along the mats in the training room. He was teaching self-defense to a room full of the base's teenagers.

He wasn't sure that what he was teaching would help them escape from a much bigger and stronger raptor, but he figured anything was better than nothing. They all deserved a chance, and he wanted to make it the best chance they could get.

The only way it could be better was if he made sure they never had to face a raptor at all.

"Come on, people." Nearby, Mac clapped her hands. "You heard the boss."

The teens moved quickly, one of each pair grabbing the wrists of their partners.

"Go," Roth called out.

He watched the straining and the grunting and groaning. It made a smile briefly flicker on his face before it dissolved in a wash of anger and annoyance. Despite the distraction of the group of kids, all he could think about was Avery.

He watched one girl struggling against her taller boyfriend. The young man was laughing, and clearly trying not to hurt her wrists. Roth stepped up and turned the girl's wrist with a gentle hand. "Like that, Clare. Now push down. Fast."

The slender girl nodded and when she got free, she did a little victory dance. "I did it!"

Her boyfriend, Leo, was grinning at her. Roth knew the pair had been found by Hell Squad, living in an underground train station in the city. Since they'd been at Blue Mountain Base, they'd both filled out and lost the gaunt, haunted look they'd had, and both smiled readily now.

"Great job, keep it up." He wandered the groups, helping and praising each pair.

"I see this is putting you in a slightly better mood," Mac said with an arched brow. She nudged him with a shoulder. "You were in a foul one this morning."

He grunted.

"You want to talk about it?"

The quiet, sincere words made him relax a little. "No. Look—"

Suddenly, the training room door slammed open and Chef hurried in, alarm stamped on his face. He searched the room, his dark gaze settling on Roth.

Frowning, Roth moved to meet the man.

"Masters, you've got to come to the kitchen."

"What? What's happened?" Roth felt a strange sense of panic, his chest contracting.

"Avery...she fell off a ladder while stocking some shelves." Chef ran a huge hand over his bald head. "Jesus, there's blood everywhere."

Roth grabbed the man's shoulders, harder than

he'd intended. "Is she okay?"

"Don't know. She bumped her head badly. She won't go to the infirmary. Keeps asking for you."

"Dammit." Roth turned to Mac. "Take over the class for me." He didn't wait to see her response, just hurried out of the room, Chef close behind him.

They didn't speak as they jogged through the tunnels toward the kitchen. Roth slammed through the door.

Shit. His pulse tripped. Avery was sitting against the wall, with what looked like a kitchen towel pressed to her head. Blood soaked the neckline of her gray tank top.

Roth hurried over and knelt beside her. "Shit, sweetheart."

She looked up at him, blinking slightly unfocused eyes. "Roth?"

His first name on her lips. He sucked in a deep breath. It felt like some sort of win in this battle of wills of theirs. He grabbed the cloth and eased it away, wincing at the wound on her scalp. "You've got a nasty gash. You need to see the doc—"

She shoved his hand away. "I remembered something." Her gaze seemed more focused now. "God." She closed her eyes for a second. "I remember the meetings with the raptors. The small raptor did all the translating. There were three meetings..."

"Okay." He wanted to know, but strangely, right now all he cared about was getting her head taken care of. "Tell me later. I'll help you to the infirmary."

"No." She slapped a hand on the floor, a twist of desperation on her face. "I might forget something. Or one of those godawful black holes might take over. I need to get this out." Her hands gripped his, her nails digging into his skin. "Please."

He pressed the cloth back to her head. She'd fight him every step of the goddamned way to the infirmary. He knew that stubborn tilt to her jaw already. "All right. Tell me."

"There were three meetings. At the first, they were just feeling us out. They didn't really demand or give much away." She rubbed a finger against her cheek, smearing blood on her skin.

Roth looked over his shoulder at Chef. "Get another clean cloth."

The big man nodded and hustled to comply, handing a freshly laundered towel to Roth.

"Go on," he told Avery. He started wiping the blood off her face.

She stared at him for a second, then gave her head a tiny shake. "At the second meeting I felt like they were showing off. They were rubbing our faces in their superior tech, showing us how powerful they were."

"Did they make any threats?"

She shook her head, winced. "No. Not then." The lines in her face deepened. "But they were setting the groundwork for it."

"What did they want?"

"They still didn't say." She released a long breath and looked at him. "Not until the third meeting."

Roth got that feeling that always crept in right before a mission went fubar. Like his chest was filling with concrete. "Go on."

"They demanded a third of the world's population."

Roth froze. "What?"

"That's what they wanted." She closed her eyes, her head falling back against the wall. "Billions of people. They wanted us to just give them billions of people."

"God." Roth tried to comprehend the words coming out of Avery's mouth and failed.

Those hazel eyes opened. "They said if we handed over the people they wanted, they'd leave. No one had to die."

Roth scraped a hand through his hair. "Hell."

"I wouldn't consider it. But the Coalition leaders ordered me to keep negotiating, to try and get the number down."

"Bastards."

"They told me they wouldn't accept any deal...that we just had to keep them busy while we looked at other options." She shook her head.

"You didn't believe them."

"No. They were hoping to get an 'acceptable' number of losses. Maybe offload criminals, and others they deemed not worthy."

Roth stood, his hands on his hips.

"I...my memories are murky after that. I was pissed. I went through the motions, but I suspect the Gizzida knew we were stalling." She sighed. "I screwed up...and billions died for it anyway." She made a choked noise, her hand resting on her thigh curled into a hard fist. "I don't remember anything after that third meeting."

"Okay, okay. That's enough. Come on, you need to see the doc." He gripped her arm and helped her to her feet.

She muttered under her breath, sagging against the wall. "Dammit. My vision is a bit blurry." Then she straightened. "Wait...I remember something else. Something I thought, but I couldn't prove."

"What?"

"The smaller raptor, the translator—" big hazel eyes met his "—I think he was a former human. I can't say what made me think that...just a few words and phrases he used. It wasn't precise enough for someone who'd learned English as a second language. It was just my gut instinct that made me think that."

God. Roth let that sink in. Perhaps the Gizzida had come earlier, and "tested" their genesis procedure on humans to ensure they were compatible. He stared at the blood-soaked cloth and then back at Avery, standing there, swaying on her feet.

He slipped an arm around her back. "Enough for now. We'll analyze it all later. Infirmary."

She huffed out a breath, taking a few unsteady steps. "God, you are bossy."

"Shut it, Stillman."

They made it into the corridor. When she cursed under her breath he frowned down at her dark head.

"Uh...my vision is really blurry now...I can barely see."

Roth cursed too. He bent and scooped her into his arms.

She made a little squeak. "I don't like being carried."

"I don't care." He stalked down the hall and moments later, slammed into the infirmary.

Doc Emerson hurried over, her white lab coat flapping around her legs and her blonde hair brushing her jaw. "Roth! What did you do to her?"

He scowled. Did people really think he'd hurt her? "Nothing—"

"Fell off a ladder," Avery said.

"Over here." Doc Emerson pushed back a curtain into an exam room. "Put her down here."

He set Avery on the bed, the pale shade of her face making his gut cramp.

"Out." The doc nudged him back, none too gently.

Roth leaned against the wall and crossed his arms.

Doc rolled her eyes. "You alpha males are all the same. Fine. Just stay out of my way."

He watched her work, hooking Avery up to a scanner, talking in a low, calm voice as she probed the head wound and asked Avery questions.

Finally, Emerson stepped back, slipping her handheld scanner into her coat pocket. "Okay. I'll start with the good news. We can seal the external wound. It's not bad, but head wounds always bleed like hell." Then the doctor's sunny face turned serious. "But the bad news is that you have some pressure building. Your brain is swelling a little. I'm going to have to give you a dose of nanomeds, but they'll fix you up in no time."

Avery leaned back against the pillows. "Do it."

The doc bustled around, grabbing items off a tray. She lifted an injector filled with a glowing, silver fluid. Roth knew it was actually microscopic medical machines that would race through the body, fixing what they could. He also knew they hurt like hell going in, and if not properly monitored, could go a little crazy and kill the patient.

As the doc prepared to inject, Roth moved closer and grabbed Avery's hand.

She turned her head, studying him for a second, then she looked back at the doc. But her fingers curled around his.

The doc depressed the injector, and Avery gritted her teeth. Roth gritted his own teeth sympathetically, and wished he could take away the pain.

"All done." Emerson patted Avery's leg. "Now I have to adjust the monitoring scanner. You just relax until the nanos are finished. If you feel any pain at any time, let me know."

Avery relaxed back against the pillows. "Doc Emerson, can I ask you a question?"

"Sure." The doctor faced them with a small smile.

"What options do you have available here for memory stimulation?"

Roth's hand flexed on hers, but she didn't look at him.

Emerson's smile evaporated like smoke. "Memory stimulation is dangerous...whatever the method."

"That wasn't my question."

Emerson shot Roth a quick glance before focusing back on Avery. "There are drugs. They have varying levels of success, and can leave you feeling like you went on a weeklong bender with a bad batch of homebrew."

"And what about electrode stimulation? Do you have the capability to carry it out?"

Emerson's lips firmed into a flat line. "That procedure is dangerous."

"But if it's necessary, the risk is worth it." Avery shifted on her pillows. "And used in conjunction with certain drugs, it can help lower the risk of side effects."

"Side effects?" Emerson said sharply. "It can damage your brain, Avery."

"I need to remember, Doc. It's important to all of us."

"No." The word burst out of Roth.

Avery turned her head. "You should be jumping for joy. The chance to unlock my memories, and learn more about the Gizzida. Learn something that could help us defeat them."

"No." He scowled.

Avery rolled her eyes. "The stoic alpha male crap doesn't fly with me, Roth." She turned back to the doctor. "Could you send all the details to my comp, please? I'll look them over and consider all the options."

The doctor looked like she wanted to argue, but gave a single nod. "I'll be back later to check on you."

Roth sat on a nearby stool. "You can think all you want. You won't do it."

"It's my decision, Masters." That stubborn chin lifted. "And you have no say in it."

Chapter Five

Avery finished bagging up some food scraps to drop off to Old Man Hamish for his compost, but her thoughts were far from the kitchen or the hydroponic gardens.

Her mind kept bouncing between whether she should risk the memory stim techniques, and of course, obsessing over Roth Masters, and that wild kiss in the dining room. The man just got under her skin...like annoying splinters.

She tied a knot in the bag. Okay, she admitted it, she was insanely attracted to him. She pressed the heels of her hands to her eyes. Why? Why did she have to be drawn to the big, annoying alpha soldier? She didn't need him. In fact, he was the last thing she needed. She needed to focus on the raptors and finding a way—any way—she could help get rid of them.

The kitchen door opened. She half expected to see Roth's large frame and scowling face, but the slim figure who crossed the kitchen was definitely not Roth.

"Hi, Avery," Elle Milton said with a smile.

Avery grabbed a towel and dried her hands. "Hi, Elle. You looking an after-dinner snack? Or is

Santha craving more sweet things?"

Elle shook her head. "Santha's probably still having cravings, but Cruz has banned me from sneaking her that homemade fudge Chef's been making." The brunette winked. "At least he thinks he's stopped me."

Avery couldn't help but smile. It seemed Hell Squad's women had worked out their own ways around their overbearing men. "So what can I help you with?"

Elle shifted a little, her face turning serious. "Noah and I have a backup memory drive in the comp lab."

"Uh-huh." Avery knew Noah Kim, the tech genius who kept the lights on and the ventilation flowing, and fixed just about every other electronic item in the base, was some sort of electronics whiz. The few times she'd seen him, the part-Australian, part-Korean man was grumpy and usually preoccupied. He reminded her of the geek squad back at Coalition Central Intelligence.

"It's a CCIA drive," Elle said.

Avery straightened. "Really?"

The other woman nodded. "We tracked the security code etched on it. We can't crack it. The encryption on it is rock-solid." Elle clasped her hands. "Do you think you can get us in?"

"I can try." Adrenaline surged through Avery's blood. The chance to be useful again, apart from peeling vegetables, made her bounce on the balls of her feet. She arched her head back. "Chef, I need to head to the comp lab. You all right by yourself?"

"Yeah, just about finished up, Av. Catch you later."

It was a quick walk to the comp lab. A sign hung on the door saying, *Shh, genius at work.*

Avery raised a brow. "What's it like working with Noah?"

Elle wrinkled her nose. "The guy can make anything electronic sit up and do his bidding. He can solve problems before I've even finished figuring out the problem to begin with, and the rest of the tech team love him."

"I hear a *but* in there."

Elle grinned. "He's super intelligent, arrogant with it, speaks his mind, and can be a bit moody."

Avery cocked her head. "Are you telling me that Marcus is never moody?"

"Oh, no. Marcus has moody down to an art form." She smiled a gentle smile. "Although he's much better lately. Happier."

And Avery could guess why. She tilted her head. "Aren't you...?" She shook her head. "Never mind."

"Oh, please ask. I don't mind."

"Aren't you afraid...for Marcus? That you'll lose him?"

Elle smiled. "Every day. But that doesn't change the fact that he's worth the worry. Every second of it."

Avery wasn't so sure.

"Anyway, Noah can swing from ecstatic over something to angry in a flash. So watch out. Oh, and if Captain Bladon is anywhere around, just duck for cover." The comms officer shook her head.

"Those two are like repelling magnets. They do not like each other, period."

"Right." Avery pushed through the door.

"Dammit to hell!" a deep male voice intoned followed by some cursing in what Avery guessed was Korean.

A piece of what might have been a comp flew past and hit the wall.

Elle thrust her hands on her hips. "Noah!"

The tall man turned. His black hair was long, brushing his shoulders, and framing a face Avery couldn't decide was handsome, interesting, hawkish, or a bit of all three. His dark eyes narrowed. "Didn't know you were going to walk in at that exact moment."

Elle stamped a foot. "Was that your half-assed attempt at an apology? I swear, you're worse than the Hell Squad guys sometimes."

Noah stalked around his desk and dropped into a beaten-up chair. He snatched something off the shelf behind him, turning it over in his fingers. Avery squinted slightly, and realized it was two small cubes—dice. The shelf was loaded with them—in all different shapes, sizes and colors.

"Sorry."

Avery smothered a laugh. That was the most grudging apology she'd ever heard.

"You were fine when I left." Elle snatched up the broken comp part and set it on a spare desk.

"I'm just peeved we can't get into this." He gestured at the slim black box on his cluttered desk. "And the Dragon called, said the comps in the prison cells aren't working…again. I don't know what the hell they do down there, but that comp was working perfectly last time I had the displeasure to be down there."

Elle shook her head. "Noah, this is Avery Stillman."

Dark, assessing eyes settled on her. "Hi."

She raised a hand.

"Avery worked for the CCIA."

Noah's gaze sharpened. "Analyst?"

"No."

He sank back in his chair, running the dice between his fingers. The move was practiced enough for her to realize he did it a lot.

"Agent, then. How high up?"

Old habits died hard. She'd never give away her secrets to someone she didn't know. Even in the middle of an alien apocalypse. "High enough to get you into that." She gestured at the drive.

"Excellent. Elle, can you set up former Agent Stillman at a desk? Get her what she needs."

"Just Avery." Why did everyone want to rub her face in her now long-gone job?

"Come on," Elle gestured toward an empty desk. "Take a seat and let me know what you need."

Soon Avery was hunched over the CCIA drive. She'd spliced it into the comp and was tapping away at the screen. She cursed loudly. The encryption was airtight. Better than almost everything she'd seen at the agency.

The only drives and comps she'd seen with this level of security held very important stuff.

She muttered and tried a work-around to circumvent the security protocols. "Come on, you little..." She huffed out a breath. Despite her frustration, she was actually enjoying this. In fact, she almost felt like herself again.

She eyed the black box, pondering her options. Maybe...yeah, that could work. She tapped the screen again, her fingers flying.

The comp beeped and data filled the screen.

"Hot damn," she said, grinning.

"You in?" Noah appeared at her shoulder, and a second later, Elle as well.

"You did it." Elle pressed a hand to her shoulder. "Well done."

The quiet praise made Avery's throat tighten. She cleared it and focused back on the screen. She hadn't realized quite how starved she'd been for some simple contact. The only person who'd touched her since she'd been pulled from that alien tank was Roth.

Noah leaned forward. He was wearing glasses now, and he shoved them higher up on his nose. "Looks like Coalition military info."

Avery peered at it, paging through the data. "It is. Specs for weapons, military combat vehicles. Shit, look. Bases as well." She paged again and stopped.

Elle gasped. "Is that Blue Mountain Base?"

"Yes." The diagrams and data listed everything about the base, as it had been before the attack.

"Who the hell was this for?" Noah pondered.

A sick feeling snaked through Avery. "Where did you find it?"

"Squad Nine found it," Noah said. "Among ruins in the city. Near a raptor installation."

A shiver sent goose bumps over Avery's skin. "You think the aliens had it?"

"I hope not." The man frowned. "They couldn't get in, surely."

Avery wasn't sure. "I wonder what else is in here."

"I'll take a look. Might be some info on the base we don't know about, or installations nearby. There's always the potential to find weapons, armor, and ammunition supplies."

"Everything helps," Elle added. "Thanks, Avery."

Avery stood. "No problem."

"Noah, you need me for anything, let me know," Elle said. "Hell Squad and Squad Nine are due back from a recon mission. I'm going to meet them."

"Got it, Elle," Noah said, his attention already on the comp on his desk. "Thanks again, Avery."

As Avery and Elle hit the corridor, Avery asked, "If Hell Squad was out, shouldn't you be on comms?"

"It was a joint mission, and not an offensive one—recon only. So only one comms officer was required," Elle answered. "Squad Nine's officer, Arden, took it."

As they got closer to where Avery needed to turn off toward the personal quarters, she heard the distant peal of alarms, and the clang of metal. The Hawk landing pads. She stared down the tunnel.

She missed the hustle and bustle that came with heading out or returning from a mission.

"Would you like to come and see the Hawks?"

Avery blinked and realized Elle was watching her. "Oh, I shouldn't, I need—"

"Come on. We both know you want to." Elle set off.

Avery stood there for a moment, torn, then she gave in and followed. It was the Hawks, that was all. She just wanted to see the Hawks.

They stepped onto the busy landing pads, and Avery breathed it all in. Overhead, from two large circular tubes cut into the rock above, two Hawk quadcopters were slowly descending. People were hurrying around, all dressed in a mishmash of uniforms and civilian clothes. The squads had been formed from whoever had survived the first wave of alien attacks—UC Navy, Army, Marines, Air force, SAS, and police officers.

A memory hit her. Her, dressed in fatigues, gesturing to her team to hurry to a waiting helicopter. She held a carbine, and the wind from the chopper made her hair dance around her face. That sense of edgy anticipation rushed through her, of knowing she was heading out to take down the bad guys. Avery blinked and the memory was gone. She took a deep breath. The blanks were slowly filling in. She just wished it wouldn't take so long.

The thought of being a part of a squad, of being out there on the front line, was so damn tempting. Her hands curled into fists by her sides.

The Hawks' skids had touched down, the rotors all slowing. The side doors slid open.

She saw Marcus Steele and his second, Cruz Ramos leap out of one Hawk.

Then she saw Roth leap out of the second Hawk.

Everything inside her went still, then quivered like it had been hit with a tuning fork. He looked hot and sweaty, his hair slicked back against his head. With his armor on, he looked even bigger, and as she watched, he started pulling pieces of the chest armor off to uncover a dark-green T-shirt, sweat-stained at the neck.

It was true, Avery thought. She had never wanted a man quite as much as she wanted Roth Masters.

Chapter Six

Avery watched other people leap off the Hawk behind Roth, and then he was surrounded by women. Armor-clad, badass-looking women. One was talking to him, gesturing as she spoke. She wasn't very tall, the top of her dark head barely reaching Roth's shoulder.

Mackenna Carides, his second-in-command. Avery hadn't seen the woman in action, but she'd heard the stories. Apparently, Carides was tough with a capital T, and could wipe the floor with anyone—even the squads' toughest soldiers.

The other women flanked them. All strong, all competently holding their carbines. One huge, silent man followed behind. He looked like a gentle giant...until you saw his dark eyes. Eyes of a warrior.

As Mac finished, a brunette with glints of red in her hair picked up the conversation. She stepped in front of Roth to stop him and make her point. She was talking fast and pissed about something.

He spent every day with these women; these strong, competent women. Avery found herself swallowing against a bitter taste in her mouth. They all looked so comfortable together. They fought side-by-side, and backed each other up, every day. She wondered if he was involved with one of them personally.

Avery tucked her hair back behind her ear. Roth didn't seem the type to do that, but the rules were more flexible now. Here at Blue Mountain Base, they didn't stand on ceremony. They didn't always use rank, or wear matching uniforms. They just did what they had to do to survive.

Arguing voices snapped her attention away from Roth. She suddenly realized a wall of very big, very tall people had approached her and Elle. A huge, rugged man was sliding an arm around Elle and tugging her close to his side.

His green eyes were on Avery though. Assessing.

"I damn well shot that alien. Right between the eyes." A tawny-haired man stood with his legs spread, his hands on his lean hips, a long-range sniper rifle tossed over one shoulder.

"Dream on, Shaw. I'd already taken him down. Three shots to the chest. That was *my* kill."

Avery's gaze swiveled to the woman squaring off in front of the sniper. She took tough to a new level. Her dark hair was in a no-nonsense braid, and she looked like she was about to slam a fist into the sniper's pretty face.

"No way." Shaw chopped a hand through the air. "You aren't stealing my kill."

"You aren't stealing *my* kill. I took down seven. You only got six." The woman glowered, and it was a scary thing.

The handsome sniper snorted, looking

unconcerned. "Dream on, Frost."

The woman made an inarticulate sound in her throat. Avery knew she was Claudia Frost, Hell Squad's only female soldier.

A tall man swung his arms around both of them. "Cool it, you two. You want to duke it out, take it down to the firing range." The man winked at Avery. "Me, I've got a woman to pry out of the lab." His gaze turned inward. "I know she'll be wearing one of those skirts that drives me crazy."

Claudia elbowed him. "Jesus, Reed. Is that all you think about, getting Natalya naked?"

Reed cocked his head. "Pretty much."

Claudia shrugged his arm off. "I'm going to grab a shower and a beer. Between Shaw's blowhard recollection of events and the rest of you getting all loved up—" she shot Marcus and Elle a hard look "—you all leave me slightly nauseated." She stalked off, her long legs carrying her out of the landing pads.

"Man, she's got more of a bug up her a—" Shaw's gaze flicked to Avery and Elle and a lazy smile appeared "—butt than usual. And I did take down that raptor."

"So did she," Cruz said, shades of Mexico in his voice.

Now the sniper scowled. "I had it under control. She didn't have to come in like Galahad and shred the fucker in the chest. She's been appearing beside me on every mission, like I'm some damn damsel in distress who needs a bodyguard."

Hell Squad all looked at each other. Marcus

cleared his throat. "We're all a bit jumpy after that aquatic alien dragged you through the ocean, tried to drown you and nearly ate you."

Avery really wanted to know what he was talking about. The sniper huffed out a breath, swiped a hand through his hair, and settled on a frustrated nod.

Just then, Squad Nine reached them. Avery looked up, her gaze clashing with Roth's. He gave her a small nod and she lifted her chin.

A man in a neat khaki uniform strode onto the landing pads. With the bit of distinguished gray at his temples, and a handsome face—not to mention the air of authority that cloaked him—he had 'man in charge' written all over him.

In the short time she'd been at base, Avery had developed a hell of a lot of respect for General Adam Holmes. He'd pulled off a miracle in creating Blue Mountain Base, keeping this many people secure, and feeding and housing them. Not to mention forming the squads and fighting back at the aliens.

She wondered if anyone else noted the lines bracketing his mouth, or the dark shadows under his eyes. The man looked like he was running on fumes.

"Steele? Masters? What did you find out there?" the general asked.

"Aliens everywhere, sir," Marcus said, his arm tightening around Elle.

"And they're acting more aggressive," Roth added.

Avery's stomach tightened. Not good.

"And it looks like they're testing new weapons." Marcus' gravelly voice did not sound happy. "Same poison they've been using but it's electrified as well."

Holmes' face twisted and he looked like he wanted to swear. "Any chance we can get our hands on some of it? Let Noah and his team take a look at it."

"We'll see what we can do," Marcus said.

Roth took a step forward. "General...it gets worse. We spotted patrols at the foothills of the Blue Mountains. My guess is they'll continue pushing our way."

Holmes' jaw tightened. "They know we're here somewhere. I'll double the base patrols." He shoved his hands on his hips. "I've also been working on a number of evacuation plans. I think it's time we start running evac simulations."

Elle gasped. "People will panic."

"I know." Holmes looked beyond exhausted, now. "I can't help that. I'd prefer them panicked, but alive. Every man, woman, and child in this base needs to know exactly what to do if the base is attacked."

"Where will we go?" The words slipped out of Avery's mouth.

Holmes' piercing blue gaze leveled on her. "I don't think we've met."

She held out a hand. "Avery Stillman."

"Stillman?" He frowned, then his brows rose. "The CCIA agent?"

"Yes, sir."

"Well, Avery, let's hope we never have to evacuate, but for now, I just need everyone to know we have a workable plan." He looked at the weary, sweat-stained soldiers. "All right, everyone dismissed. Clean up and get some rest."

Hell Squad and Squad Nine started moving out, murmuring and patting each other on the back. Avery caught the Squad Nine women eyeing her with undisguised curiosity as they passed.

"Marcus, I don't think you've met Avery," Elle said.

He lifted his chin. "So, you're Masters' favorite interrogation target."

Avery rolled her eyes. "The guy is persistent." She glanced Roth's way. He was standing near the doorway, talking with his squad. He hadn't looked her way as he was leaving, and she felt her shoulders slump a little.

"You really don't remember anything?" Marcus asked.

She shrugged. "Some of it's coming back. Slowly."

"Avery just helped Noah and I access a CCIA drive," Elle said. "Lots of interesting info on there."

Marcus studied Elle's face before his piercing gaze fell on Avery again. "If Masters gets to be too much, let me know. I'll handle it."

Avery straightened. "I appreciate the offer, but I can handle Roth just fine." She saw that he and the others in Nine were now gone. "I should be off. Elle, I'll see you later."

"Sure, Avery. Thanks again for your help today."

"Nice to meet you, Marcus. And thanks for the work you do out there."

Marcus inclined his head.

Avery wandered the tunnels, not really sure where she was headed. She was thinking about the inhabitants having to abandon the base. If it came to that, some wouldn't make it—the injured, the elderly, the very young. She thumped a fist against her head. She needed to remember.

She had to remember something that would help avoid an evacuation.

She turned toward the personal quarters and ended up at Roth's door.

After a few minutes of trying to talk herself out of it, she knocked.

It took a moment, but finally it was yanked open. "Mac, I said I'm not up for a beer—" Spotting her, he broke off.

For a long moment, they simply stared at each other.

Avery opened her mouth to speak, but she was having trouble breathing, and no words would come out.

Roth had clearly just stepped out of the shower. The only thing he wore was a towel wrapped around his lean hips, leaving everything else bare.

Holy hell, the man was ripped. His arms were huge, his shoulders hard, his pecs sculpted, and his abdomen...it was ridge after ridge of muscle. Avery shifted, trying to quell the hungry feeling inside. She watched a small droplet of water that clung to the hair on his chest. It broke free, traveling downward over taut bronze skin and even tauter muscles.

"Avery?"

She jerked her eyes to his. "I…wanted to talk."

He stepped back, holding the door open wider.

She walked into his quarters. They were much the same as hers. Bed against one wall, small kitchenette tucked in the back, and a tiny living area with a sagging couch. There was a door she knew would lead to a compact bathroom.

She wandered in and eyed the tablet on the coffee table. It displayed an old sports e-magazine on laser ball. "You're a fan?"

"I was."

Right. Because there was no laser ball league anymore. All the stadiums would be empty, the players dead. "I loved laser ball. Played when I was at school." Based on American football, it incorporated a powered ball and shoes. Players ran faster, threw farther and jumped higher. "One of my foster fathers was the coach of a high school team. We used to watch all the games." Her throat tightened. She'd let herself get too attached to Mr. Lee, and it had hurt when she'd been shifted to another home. She wondered if he was still alive and was shocked at the flash of grief that stole her breath.

"Hey." A warm hand brushed her cheek. "You okay?"

She nodded and turned, to find her nose almost buried in that hard chest that kept pulling her gaze in like a magnet. He was too close. "We should toss a laser ball sometime. Bet I could score in under five minutes."

Roth snorted. "My father was a professional coach. I got a university scholarship on laser ball."

Her eyes widened. "Really? Did you ever consider going pro?"

"Yeah." He paused, his face hardening. "But...my family was killed during my freshman year, and I dropped out."

"Oh. I'm sorry." She didn't remember the drug addict mother who'd given her up. She imagined losing a loving family you'd had your entire childhood was devastating. "Car accident?"

"No. They were at the Mount Brookside Shopping Plaza."

Cold washed over her. Mount Brookside had been a terrorist attack. The shopping center had been raided by armed gunmen, then bombs had detonated. "God, Roth, I really am sorry."

His face was composed, but those pale eyes glittered. "Thanks. After that, playing ball didn't seem so important. I joined the Army."

God, he'd given up his dream to fight for his country. To battle terrorists. She felt something inside her crumble. She took a step backward. "I'm going to try the memory stimulation—"

Roth scowled, crossing his arms over his chest. "We've been over this. No."

She scowled back. God, couldn't the man put some clothes on? "My body, my brain, my decision. I have to do something, Roth. I have to help." She spun away, taking a deep breath. "I'm useless like this, all these broken memories. Medical won't clear me to fight—"

"You were in that tank for who knows how long, Avery. I know I was pushing you before, but now I think you just need more time."

Time they didn't have. She straightened and looked him directly in the eye. "The alien troops are back on the streets, getting closer to this base. Will they wait for my head to fill in the blanks?"

His mouth firmed into a line.

She closed the few steps between them. "We both know how it will go down if the base is overrun. People will die." Her breath hitched. "And so many are already dead."

He gripped her shoulders, his thumbs brushing over her collarbones. "I know you think that's on you, but it isn't."

"I was head of the negotiations, Roth. My responsibility."

He cursed and shook her a little. "Let it go."

"I can't." A harsh whisper and she felt something inside her break. "I messed up, I have to make up for it somehow."

"Avery—"

"All I can do is try the memory stim and pray that I can give you some intel that might help us keep the base safe and push back at the aliens."

"Dammit." His fingers tightened on her skin. "Why do you always have to fight everything I say?"

Anger sparked, hot and righteous. "Because

sometimes you don't listen! That head of yours can be pretty hard."

With a warning tone, he backed her up a few steps. "Avery—"

"Don't tell me to let it go, that it isn't my fault. The same would apply to your family."

He stiffened. "My family has nothing to do with this."

"Don't tell me you didn't feel guilty that they died and you didn't. That you didn't do something to save them. You gave up everything to join the military and fight for them." She lowered her voice. "I have to do the same."

His blue eyes turned to steel. Her back hit the wall and her throat suddenly went dry, but she stood her ground.

And found herself pinned to the wall by Roth's body.

Then he cursed and slid his hands under her bottom. Helpless to resist, she wrapped her legs around his waist, and his hard cock pressed firmly against her. They both groaned.

"Damn," he muttered. "You've crawled under my skin. I think of you every damn minute of the day. Even on my missions, when I should be focused on other things."

His confession, delivered in that deep growl, made her shudder, her hands sinking into his shoulders. He was only covered by that thin towel, and a part of her was desperate to see him. She wanted to stroke her hands all over him—his hard chest, his thick thighs, the long cock she felt against her.

Roth cursed again, and then one of his hands was under her shirt, cupping her breast, kneading.

"This is crazy," she whispered. "Half the time we don't like each other, and the rest of the time—"

"And the rest of the time, we both want to tear each other's clothes off." He tweaked her nipple between his fingers making her moan.

"Damn you, yes," she hissed.

"Nothing wrong in finding some pleasure, Avery."

Because she couldn't stop herself, she rubbed against him, saw his eyes flare. "I know. But generally I prefer to like my lovers."

His hand slid lower, and then it was between them, shoving her skirt up. When a long finger slid against the edge of her panties, she made a small noise, her hips tipping forward.

"You like me, sweetheart. Even if you won't admit it."

He pushed her panties to the side, his finger running through her folds. She was embarrassingly wet for him.

He groaned. "Sweetheart. So wet, so perfect. I can't wait to put my mouth here, lap you all up."

His words made her belly clench. "Roth—"

Without warning, he slid one blunt finger inside her. She arched again, made a keening cry.

"You like that," he growled. His thumb brushed through her curls, found her clit.

She made another choked cry. The sensations

storming through her were glorious. "Yes. God, it's been so long since anyone's touched me."

"I'll touch you, baby," he murmured.

Then suddenly, she was pulled away from the wall and he was carrying her, striding toward the couch. He dropped her on the over-soft cushions. Then he tugged her toward the edge, spreading her legs and kneeling between them on the floor.

Avery had the fleeting thought that she should say something, do something. But he ripped her panties away and left her spread there, bare for him to see, and she couldn't form any words. She felt like she was in a sensual storm, unable to do anything except just hold on for the ride.

No, dammit. She wanted him to enjoy this, too. She reached for him.

"Uh-uh." He shook his head, lowering to nip her hipbone.

"Roth." Her hips lifted. "I want to touch you."

"You will. But right now, I want to lap at those pretty pink lips of yours and suck on that little clit until you cry out my name." His ice-blue eyes blazed. "You going to call out my name, Avery? So loud my neighbors will know exactly what I'm doing to you?"

Her breath hitched. "Yes."

He lowered his head and his tongue slid through her damp folds.

Oh, God. Her hands clamped in his hair. It had been so long since she'd felt pleasure, since she'd had an insanely attractive man pleasuring her.

Avery gave herself up to the cascade of feelings.

She felt her release thundering closer, making every muscle in her body tighten to the breaking point. He lapped at her like he needed her taste just to survive, all his concentration on his task.

He looked up at her, and she watched as his tongue licked her flesh. He kept eye contact as he tongued her clit, then he broke their gaze to tilt his head and suck the small nub into his mouth. "Christ, you are hot, Avery."

Too much. Pleasure slammed into her, her climax tearing through her body. Her back arched, and she felt Roth's hands gripping her thighs, holding her in place. She screamed his name.

When she could think again, she felt like a warm puddle. She looked at him. He still knelt between her legs, his head bowed. She pressed a hand to his cheek. "Roth?"

He looked up and her stomach tightened. Desire was burning white-hot in his eyes, his face set in stark lines of need.

Impossibly, desire sparked in her sated body. This man seemed to wrench so many emotions out of her, and she couldn't understand it.

She slithered off the couch and onto her knees beside him. The towel was still around his hips, but had slipped down a few inches, revealing more of the hard muscle of his stomach. She licked her lips. And the towel was tented impressively.

She tore it away.

She drew in a breath. As she took his large cock in her hand, he groaned. So big. She stroked it, and when he groaned again, her gaze went to his face.

That look, that stark look of need, was all for her.

Suddenly, a beeping noise penetrated her pleasure-fuzzed head.

Roth cursed and pulled away. "I have to take that. That's the general's ringtone."

As she watched, Roth hitched the towel around himself again, and Avery suddenly felt chilled. She tugged her clothes into place and looked around for her missing panties, but they were nowhere to be seen.

Roth stabbed a button on his communicator. "General."

"Masters. The debrief started five minutes ago. Where are you?"

Avery watched as color filled Roth's cheeks.

"Sorry, sir, just finishing...cleaning up in my quarters. I'll be there in three." As he ended the call, he turned to Avery. "Sorry."

She shook her head. "Duty calls." And maybe it was a sign. There was an alien war going on. She couldn't afford to have Roth Masters messing her up. This...attraction between them was just a distraction. "It was a great little interlude. Let's leave it at that."

"Avery..."

She hurried to the door. "Don't sweat it." *Keep it casual, Avery. Easy*. She winked at him. "And I owe you a blow job."

Roth made a growling sound. He charged at her, and damn the man could move. She dodged, but she wasn't fast enough. She found herself caught between the wall and Roth's bare chest once more.

His hands were pressed to the wall on either side of her head. "This was not some simple roll in the hay."

"No, it was oral sex on your couch."

He growled again. "So, you're going to keep throwing walls between us."

"There is no 'us', Roth. Most of the time, you don't even like me."

Something softened in his face. "You've got that wrong, sweetheart. I like everything about you, even your prickly stubbornness. And I really enjoy hearing you cry out my name when you come."

Now Avery felt heat in her cheeks. "You have to go, remember?"

Frustration tightened his jaw. "Yes, dammit, I do."

"I'm doing the memory stimulation, Roth."

A muscle ticked in his jaw. "Then I want to be there when you do."

Her belly quivered. No one had ever been with her at her health checks growing up. A social worker, sure, but no one who'd ever wanted to be there. "Okay."

"Promise me."

"Yes." A knot of tension that she hadn't realized had been lodged in her belly unraveled a little. That was Roth Masters; he'd do the right thing, even when he disagreed.

She pushed against him, and he stepped back. As she opened the door, she realized she didn't want to leave. She shook her head. *Don't be stupid, Avery. Don't get attached.*

Suddenly, she was spun around and a hard mouth slammed down on hers. His tongue thrust between her lips, and Avery threw her arms around him and kissed him back. Then she was dragging her mouth over his jaw, down his neck. Something wild called to her and she bit down on the hard tendons. He growled, his arms curling around her.

They parted, panting.

"God, go, before I tell the general and his debrief to go to hell and drag you to my bunk."

She straightened. "Maybe I'd drag you to my bunk. And I'd be on top, Masters." She shot him a smile. "I like the top."

He swatted her butt. "Go." A fierce growl.

As Avery hurried down the tunnel, she felt a lightness for the first time since she'd been pulled from that tank.

Chapter Seven

Avery shifted in the armchair, trying not to bump all the cords attached to her. She couldn't seem to get comfortable.

"One more." Doc Emerson leaned over and pressed a sticky electrode pad to Avery's bare shoulder.

One more. Right. There were already a bunch of other ones sticking to her temples, neck, arms and chest. She wore a tight tank top to give the doc better access. She shifted again, hating that she couldn't settle down.

The doc pressed a hand to Avery's shoulder and squeezed. "Relax. Are you sure you want to do this? You know I'm against the idea."

Avery gave a jerky nod. Roth had promised to be here. She'd left a message on his comp, telling him the doc had set up a time for the memory stim procedure. The doc started tapping on a scanner screen nearby, and Avery let her head drop back against the chair. It was one they used for the regular blood donations all the base residents had to give. Well, except her, and the other alien-lab survivors. The doc was being cautious, not letting them donate until she could fully rule out anything the aliens had put in their blood. Blood that was needed for anyone who was injured...which she guessed was most often the squad soldiers.

She glanced at the door, but saw no sign of wide shoulders and a sandy head. Maybe Squad Nine got called out? Or maybe he'd forgotten and had better things to do.

She straightened. She wasn't a little girl, needing someone to hold her hand. "Let's get this show on the road, Emerson."

The doctor turned and held up a pressure injector. "Okay. I have a few different drugs I need to give you. I'll just be a minute."

Emerson bustled around. The scanner started a steady beat, and Avery watched various lines on the screen, bobbing and dipping.

"The drugs are pretty potent, Avery." Emerson's face turned serious. "I have to warn you. In order to stimulate your memories, the drugs will lower your inhibitions."

Avery's hands clenched the armrests. She thought of her faceless mother, snorting drugs, injecting them, desperate for another hit. That was what she'd come from. "I'll...have no control?"

"They won't make you do things you really don't want to do. They just take the brakes off the things you want to do but stop yourself from doing."

Avery released a slow breath. "I've always wanted to learn to tango. Hopefully I won't be dipping and turning around your infirmary with a rose clenched between my teeth."

Emerson laughed. "There you go. Don't worry.

I'm here, I'll make sure things don't get out of hand."

Avery nodded and Emerson went back to organizing her equipment. The doctor shoved a portable light closer, the glare spearing into Avery's eyes, and a pain gripped her head.

A memory, harsh and hungry, hit her. She tensed. She heard raptors, was being dragged across the floor, and she was yelling. Raptor grunts echoed in the darkness...along with human screams. Orange light filtered through the room, giving the place a scary feel and ahead she saw the empty tank waiting for her.

She heard a female voice calling her name, a hand shaking her shoulder. Avery ignored it. She wanted to remember, but now her heart was beating like a giant drum, reverberating in her head and she...was afraid.

"Avery."

Roth's deep, steady voice made her blink.

She realized he was kneeling in front of her, his big hands covering hers on the armrests. The memory of the alien lab shrank in a flash, like he'd frightened it away. "Roth?"

"I'm here, sweetheart." One of his hands slid up her arm, rubbing. "What did you remember?"

She shuddered and pressed her head against the plump armchair. "Being dragged toward that tank." She shook her head. "Keep going, Doc."

Emerson looked like she wanted to argue, but with a sigh, she pressed an injector to Avery's neck. "The first lot of drugs."

Avery focused on Roth. He stayed kneeling, but she could see he was wearing his armor on the lower half of his body, and just a T-shirt on the top. His hair was a little mussed, no doubt thanks to his combat helmet. "You had a mission."

"Just base patrol. Got waylaid in the handover to the next team, that's why I was a bit late."

She wasn't going to tell him she was glad he was here. But she wanted to.

Her gaze zeroed in on a dark shadow on his neck. A bruise. Oh, God. "Is that a hickey?"

His hand went to his neck and he grinned. "Yeah, a hot little wildcat marked me."

Avery's mouth dropped open. She'd done that. Left that mark on him. She was equal parts embarrassed and pleased.

"Caught hell for it at my debriefing." He rolled his eyes. "Don't get me started on my squad. Don't think they'll ever let me live it down."

"I can heal that for you, Roth," Emerson said with a wide smile.

He thumbed the mark again. "No, thanks. I kind of like it."

Emerson snorted and turned back to Avery. When the doctor winked, Avery had to fight the urge to laugh.

"Okay, second lot of drugs, Avery." Emerson hesitated with the injector. "I won't lie, these drugs are going to hurt."

"Do it." Avery felt the dual sensations, the cool press of the injector on her neck and the warm press of Roth's fingers on her arms.

The drugs went in, and it felt like fire in her veins. She arched against the chair, wincing.

"Shit, Doc, should it hurt that much?" Roth demanded.

"It'll wear off shortly," Emerson answered.

"It's okay, Avery." Roth patted her hands. "You're tough enough to handle it."

"I'm tough enough to take you on, so yeah, I guess you're right."

A crooked smile appeared on his rugged face. "You'd only take me down if you got lucky."

She snorted. "You're dreaming, Masters. You're all brute strength, I'm skill."

"Sounds like a challenge to me." His fingers brushing her arm gentled. "Well, you certainly aren't brute anything, although there is plenty of strength under your prickly persona."

"I'm not prickly."

He made a masculine sound that she translated to a skeptical "yeah, right."

Emerson interrupted. "Avery, I'm going to ask you some standard questions, just answer truthfully. Then we'll ask the questions referencing the aliens."

"Got it."

"What's your full name?" Emerson asked.

"Avery Lauren Stillman."

"Lauren," Roth murmured. "Pretty."

"Occupation."

A feeling of lassitude was starting to flow through her, the pain receding. She snuggled back into the chair. She felt warm and calm. God, it felt good. She hadn't felt like this…well, except for those moments in Roth's arms. She looked at him now, her gaze boring into his blue eyes.

"Avery, what's your occupation?" Emerson asked again.

"I'm a special agent with the Coalition Central Intelligence Agency." She frowned. "No, that's not right. I was, but I'm not anymore. Now I work in the kitchen."

"How are you feeling?" Emerson studied whatever the scanner screen was displaying.

Avery smiled. "Pretty darn good." She giggled. "Awesome."

"High as a kite," Roth muttered.

"Like I said, your inhibitions are lowered. It'll make it easier for you to recall the memories you're after." Emerson turned. "Where are you from?"

"Brisbane, originally."

"What were your parents' names?"

"I don't know. I never knew them."

The doctor paused for a second. "Neither of them?"

"My mother was apparently a drug addict. She gave me up as soon as I was born."

"Who did you live with?"

"I lived in foster homes. Fifteen of them."

Avery heard Emerson gasp and Roth curse. His hands tightened on her.

"It wasn't all doom and gloom. Most of the homes were good. Good food, clean clothes, they made sure I went to school. It inspired me to want more from my life. I wanted a career, I wanted to be important, I wanted to help and I wanted to be in charge of my life."

"All right," Emerson said. "Let's move on. One more question, Avery. Who are your closest friends?"

"Friends? No one. I don't have any and I didn't really have any before the invasion. I was too busy at work, and I traveled a lot."

"Lovers?" Roth growled.

"Roth," Emerson admonished, but they both ignored her.

Avery smiled, she thought it felt goofy. "No one special. Just a few casual ones here and there. I never wanted the hassle of a man to boss me around and moan that I didn't give him enough attention." She eyed Roth, wondering why he looked so pleased. "Besides, caring for people is a stupid move. They always leave. Why set yourself up for the pain?"

Roth's face went hard. His gaze roamed her face. "Sweetheart."

"I never really wanted anyone enough...until I saw you."

Something flared in Roth's eyes. "Doc?"

"I'm adjusting the levels, looks like the drugs have hit her system a bit hard."

"That big hard body of yours, all those muscles." Avery grinned. "Hard for a woman to ignore. But I also like your drive, your determination. It makes me want to climb all over you."

Beside her, Avery heard Emerson stifle a laugh.

"Avery," Roth's voice was a ragged growl. "Stop

talking. Doc, fix the levels. She's going to kill me after this."

"Don't be mean to the doc." Avery slapped a hand at his chest, missed, and clipped his chin, instead. As he scowled at her and grabbed her hand in his, she smiled. "At least I know now what that tongue of yours can do."

"Really?" Emerson said. "Want to share that?"

"No." Roth leaned forward and pressed his mouth to Avery's.

Mmm. Avery moved into him, opening her mouth to drink him in. Oh, the man could kiss.

"Enough." Emerson slapped Roth's shoulder, and he drew back. "I need her calm, and you're making her heart rate spike." She nodded at the screen where a line was moving like crazy.

Avery settled back in her chair.

"All right," Roth said. "Let's go back to before the alien invasion."

"Do we have to?" Avery complained. She felt so good, she didn't want to think about the aliens.

"You were meeting with the Gizzida," Roth said.

Now a chill swept through Avery, wiping away the humming desire. "Yes."

***

Roth stayed close to Avery, watching her face. Emerson had warned him before that if the memory stim went wrong, she could have a seizure or fall into a coma. The slightest sign of discomfort and he was pulling the plug.

He'd been battling to find out what Avery knew, and now...now he was torn. He didn't want this woman hurt, and he hated that she had to go through this.

"The negotiations had stalled. The Gizzida were getting impatient." Avery's voice had become a flat monotone. A crease appeared in the middle of her forehead and she rubbed at her temple.

"What is it?" he asked.

"Something...I discovered something?"

"About the aliens?"

She shook her head. "No...it was about...the Coalition President."

Roth pulled back, surprised. "President Howell?"

Her eyes widened. "Yes. He had a backup plan. He hadn't shared it, was keeping it very top secret. I discovered documents on it."

"What?"

"The Coalition were building...they were building..." Her brow scrunched more. "Dammit, I can't remember."

"Don't push it too hard." He rubbed her arm. "It'll come."

She looked at him. "I find you insanely attractive."

God, she was going to kill him. "Right back at you."

"I don't do relationships. They are hazardous to people's health."

"Only if you do them with the wrong people."

"You think we're right for each other?" She made a noise in her throat. "You're all alpha and bossy.

We'd kill each other in about ten minutes."

"But we'd have awesome sex before we did." But he knew she was right. He knew others in the squads had relationships, but Roth couldn't risk it. He couldn't drop the ball or his focus.

"Hello, don't forget I'm right here listening to all this," Emerson muttered.

Avery laughed, then her eyes went wide. "I remember. They were building an underground bunker."

Roth struggled to pull his focus off imagining sex with Avery and back to the questioning. "A bunker. To shelter in?"

She nodded.

"Not in a military base?" It seemed crazy the Coalition would ignore Blue Mountain Base, when it was right on their doorstep.

"No, somewhere else. Somewhere underground." She grimaced. "South of Sydney. They planned to take a select group there to ensure the survival of the human race. Top scientists, artists, government officials."

Roth fought back a curse. Select an important, privileged few to survive, and screw the rest of the world.

Avery's mouth tightened. "I didn't like it. I felt they weren't giving everything to negotiations that could save the entire world." She rubbed her temple again, vigorously. "There was something else, something important. What was it?" She pressed both hands to the side of her head. "I don't remember. I *have* to remember."

"Easy. Stay calm."

"No. I have to remember." The last word was shouted.

He got in her face. "No, you have to stay calm, Avery."

Then she gasped, like she couldn't breathe. "President Howell. I was in his office. I saw documents…"

"What were they?"

"He was having private meetings with the Gizzida."

"What?" Roth breathed. He sensed Emerson stiffen.

"He was meeting with them…to bargain for his own safety and a small group of his selection."

"To live in this bunker?"

She nodded. "I confronted him. I was so damned angry. And…"

"And…"

She pulled her hands from Roth and curled them against her chest. "He sold me out. To the Gizzida."

"Jesus." Roth wanted to slam his knuckles into something, anything, and rage at the sky. His hands curled into fists. "What happened?"

"At our next meeting, he organized for me to be alone with them. They took me."

Roth heard a tremor in her voice.

"Her vitals are getting a little elevated, Roth," Emerson said quietly.

He gripped her ankles, rubbing the soft skin there. "It's okay, Avery. You're free now."

"And billions are dead. Because I didn't see

through Howell's rotten exterior. I could have kept negotiating, working with the Gizzida."

"They're here for humans, Avery. They were never going to leave without a significant number of bodies for their tanks."

Her bottom lip trembled before she firmed it. "They put me in a cage." Her voice was flat again. "I was hungry. Thirsty." She shivered. "There were other humans in cages, too."

"Where?" Roth asked, resisting the urge to pound his fists into the floor.

"The dome. I remember the orange light. That damned orange light that made it all seem like a bad dream. Or a fucking nightmare." She made a choking sound. "We were all in cages, and I could see the tanks. They were growing them...to put us in them."

"Enough." Roth got to his feet. "That's enough."

She moved, quick as lightning, tugging the electrode cables behind her before her hands gripped his wrists. "No. There's something else."

"I said, enough."

"I have to remember," she said, frantically. Her nails bit into his skin. "Howell, he gave the Gizzida something else. Information in return for his safety."

Shit. "What?"

"He gave them military information. Our weapons, our vehicles, our troop training. There were a series of CCIA hard drives he handed over."

Every muscle in Roth's body froze. "No."

Her face was etched with despair. "Roth, it

included information on the bases. And...Blue Mountain Base was in there. It was why he had to build his bunker somewhere else. He gave them the base schematics, the power systems, the weapons...everything."

"Oh, God," Emerson said, gripping the scanner.

Avery's wild hazel eyes met Roth's. "They know where we are."

Suddenly her back arched and a short scream escaped her mouth.

"Emerson!" Roth reared up, pulling Avery into his arms. She was shaking spasmodically, her eyes rolling back in her head.

"A seizure." The doctor ran her handheld scanner over Avery. "Get her on the table."

He lifted Avery up, heedless of the electrodes being yanked off. She was jerking so hard in his arms, he had to exert a lot of strength to hold on to her.

He got her on the exam table. "Come on, Avery."

With a grim face, Emerson set to work. She pressed an injector to Avery's neck. "Hold her, so she doesn't fall off."

Roth already was. "Will the injection stop this?"

"It should." Emerson's gaze met Roth's.

"What aren't you saying?" he bit out.

"If this goes on too long, it could do irreversible damage to her brain."

No. Roth stared down at the woman beneath his hands. She'd called to him from the moment she squared off with him, dripping wet, in an alien lab. He hadn't let himself give in to the attraction, not completely, but now knowing he might never get the chance…his lungs constricted. "Help her."

Emerson ran her portable scanner over Avery. "She has to help herself."

She was a fighter. As her body jerked against his hands, he gritted his teeth. He should never have let her do this procedure.

Suddenly, she went still, her body dropping limply down against the table.

Emerson let out a breath. "She's stable."

Roth brushed at Avery's dark hair, hoping Emerson didn't notice that his hands were unsteady. Avery's face was pale, her lashes dark against her cheeks. So still, all the fierceness gone. "How come she's not waking up?"

"Coma was always a risk."

His hands tightened on Avery's silky hair. "You're saying she might never wake up?"

"I can't give you absolutes, Roth. But I can tell you her vitals are stable, she's young, fit, and strong. She'll likely wake up within the hour."

He brushed a thumb over her temple. "I have to meet with the general. Pass on the information." He couldn't delay that.

Emerson nodded. "Go."

He hated having to leave Avery. "You'll take care of her?"

The doctor's face softened. "Of course."

He brushed his lips over Avery's. "I'll be back," he whispered. He forced himself to head for the door. "Call me when she's awake."

Chapter Eight

"No." General Holmes dropped heavily into a chair at the conference table in the base's Operations Area.

Roth nodded. "They have information on Blue Mountain Base. Our military capabilities. Our systems. Our location. Everything."

"Fuck me." Marcus Steele raked a hand over his head.

Tane Rahia, leader of Squad Three, stood silent, his face looking as though it were carved from stone.

"The Coalition would never go for something like this," Holmes said.

"It sounds like Howell acted on his own. There's no way to know how many others he sold out, like Avery, who discovered and opposed his little escape plan." If Howell had been there, Roth would have taken great pleasure in slamming a fist into the politician's square jaw.

"We aren't safe here," Marcus said.

Holmes planted his hands on the table's glossy surface. "The raptors haven't attacked the base. Not once in eighteen months. Maybe they never got the information? Roth, maybe that hard drive you found was data the aliens lost."

Roth didn't respond. They all knew it was wishful thinking. They couldn't risk lives on wishes and dreams.

"The aliens have been hanging around the mountains, but never coming close enough to spook us off." Tane's voice was smooth and deep, with the hint of a New Zealand accent in it. The man's Maori heritage was obvious in his strong face and darker skin. His black hair was pulled back in dreadlocks that would have never been code in the military. Tane, and all his squad—known as the Berserkers—hadn't been military. Mercenaries, bounty hunters, bikers—they were all rough, badass, and damn good fighters, if a little crazy and prone to never following orders.

"They know we're here," Marcus agreed.

Holmes dragged in a breath and nodded. The man looked beyond tired. "Okay, they haven't attacked yet...so we aren't going to go off half-cocked and rush out of here. We need to step up the evacuation drills, make sure all the residents have it down pat. And I want all squads pulling extra shifts for recon for escape routes and alternative shelter locations."

"And more base patrols," Roth suggested.

The general nodded again. "Yeah. We have to know the second a raptor steps foot within an inch of the base perimeter." He tapped his fingers on the table. "I'll step up the prep work on Operation Swift Wind."

Swift Wind was the top secret evac and escape

plan the general was working on. Roth had only heard parts of it, but his respect for the general had risen another notch. The guy was smart, and he wanted everyone in the base to make it if they had to leave.

"Nowhere is as safe or as well set up as Blue Mountain Base," Tane said. "It'll be hard to find a good alternative."

"That's just it, Tane," the general replied. "The base isn't safe anymore, but if we rush out before we're ready, not everyone will make it."

"Stay here and everyone might die." Roth knew it was what they were all thinking.

"Then let's hope whatever it is that's holding the raptors from attacking keeps them at bay a little longer." Holmes rubbed the back of his neck, then straightened. "But like I said, more base patrols, more recon, and I'll talk to Noah. We need more drones in the air, as well. We won't let these bastards sneak up on us. And the priority needs to be a safe alternative."

Roth stared hard at the other men before his gaze settled on the general. "There is one possible safe place we could go."

The general frowned. "Where?"

"Avery said Howell outfitted an underground bunker. No idea how big it is, or how many it's already holding…but it would be better than caves or burned-out buildings with no power or water."

The general nodded, his gaze distant. "It's a possibility. But we don't know where it is."

"South of the city, somewhere."

Elle, who'd been sitting quietly by a comp, swiveled in her chair and started tapping at her comp screen. "Let me pull up a map of the area and isolate any underground installations that could be prime candidates for conversion to a bunker."

The large screen on the wall filled with an aerial map.

"Nothing military," Roth said. "He sold all military info to the raptors."

"Bastard." Tane's voice held no inflection...which made it sound even scarier.

A handful of dots appeared on the screen. Elle was frowning. "Old railway tunnels."

Holmes frowned. "When were they built?"

"The late 1800s," Elle answered. "They were all closed after about thirty years. They were very steep and narrow."

The general shook his head. "Don't sound like promising prospects."

"The rest of the options are all underground coal mines."

Roth frowned, too. "A mine wouldn't be very comfortable."

"And most of these mines were longwall coal mines. They used high-tech equipment to support the roof above, and used large shearing machines to mine the coal in long slices. They would have chewed through large panels of coal, leaving empty space behind it."

The general frowned, tapping his fingers again. "But it would have been unstable afterward, right?"

"Sure," Elle said. "But Howell would have had

some time, and of course the resources and money, to turn that mined-out space into something safe and useable."

Holmes nodded. "He would have thrown a lot of money and resources at it. Decking out a mine may not have been that hard. There would have been some utilities already in place."

"I need to go in and get a closer look. See if anything stands out," Roth said.

Holmes nodded. "It's too late to go today. First thing tomorrow morning, take the Darkswifts."

In his head, Roth already started planning the mission.

"I'm coming."

The familiar voice had him spinning. Avery stood in the doorway. She looked okay. A little pale and shaky, but that fierce, fighting look was back in her eyes.

"Ms. Stillman, how are you feeling?" Holmes said, standing.

"Like I just got dropped from a quadcopter, but I'll be fine soon enough." She took a step forward and when she wobbled, Roth closed the distance in two large strides.

"You pick me up and I'll punch you," she hissed under her breath.

"Cool it." He gripped her arm and helped her to a chair.

She faced the general. "I'm trained. I might have more information about Howell's bunker that I could remember if I see the area. I can help."

"The medical team haven't cleared you—"

"Because of my patchy memories. I have most of those back now." Her chin lifted a notch. "I need to help."

Roth heard frank honesty in her voice. Avery Stillman was a straight shooter all the way.

The general considered her, then his tapping fingers stopped. "Roth's in charge of the mission. It's his call."

Her head turned, her gaze hitting him.

He sucked in a deep breath. The caveman part of his brain was shouting at him to keep her safe. That part of his brain remembered what it felt like to lose his family in one violent act of terror.

The rest of him knew Avery could be a vital part of this mission. He had to use her.

He'd be with her. By her side the entire time. He'd keep her safe, no matter what.

"You're in."

***

Avery stood in the doorway to the small office and watched Roth work. He was completely absorbed in planning his mission.

He pushed some maps on the desk aside and scribbled some notes on a tablet. He leaned forward, his desk chair squeaking a little, circled a location on the map, and then sank back. He looked up and finally noticed her.

"How long have you been there?" he said.

"Long enough." She stepped inside and closed the door. "Nice digs."

He shrugged. "It's barely bigger than a closet, but it's a space where I can sit in silence and plan. Sometimes my squad gets pretty opinionated when we're planning a mission."

Apart from the desk and the chair, there was a small bookcase and one lone poster on the wall. It was from the last laser ball championship. It had been torn and taped back together. "So, you mean this is somewhere you can hide from them?"

His lips quirked. "Hide is a strong word."

Avery dragged a finger over the wooden desk. God, he looked delectable sitting there, his shirt open and showing a tempting triangle of hard chest. That crease of concentration on his rugged face.

"How are you feeling?" he asked.

"Fine. All the effects of the drugs have worn off." She felt a pinch of embarrassment. "Ah...I said some things..."

"Don't sweat it, Avery. You weren't yourself."

She always tried to be honest. With herself, most of all. "I meant everything I said."

His nostrils flared and he watched her steadily. "That part about wanting me more than you've wanted anyone before—"

"True." She stepped between him and the desk, and leaned against the wood. "I've realized we have to enjoy the moment. We could all be dead tomorrow."

He parted her legs, his hands sliding along her thighs. "Avery, I'm not interested in being some faceless fuck." He gripped the hem of her shirt, fiddled with it.

His fingers brushed her belly, and she sucked in a breath. She felt that small touch all the way through her. "I thought you soldiers liked the soldier bunnies that flit around base trying to get your attention."

"Some do. Nothing wrong with that." He slipped his hands under her shirt, sliding up to cup her breasts.

God. She bit down on her lip and arched into his rough palms. He flicked his thumbs over her nipples, and she felt them pebble under his touch.

"I want more," he murmured. "I seem to have acquired a taste for prickly personalities and fierce determination."

"We're in the middle of an alien apocalypse, Roth. We can't have more. Hell, relationships hardly lasted before the apocalypse, now they're even more precarious."

He cocked his head. "Afraid?"

Her heart jumped. "Of you? No."

He tweaked her nipples again, making her moan. "Of this. Of what's between us."

She framed his face and their eyes met. She felt fire over her skin and saw the answering flames in his gaze.

No, she wasn't afraid to dance with fire. She was deathly afraid she'd come to love it and then it would be taken away from her.

Stop thinking, Avery. Just touch him, taste him, take him.

She moved and he did too. He closed his mouth

over hers, and the kiss was hot and hard, riding an edge close to punishing.

"Door," he said against her lips.

"I already locked it." She pulled him closer, tongues thrusting, and Roth slipped his hands around her back, down to the top of her ass and slid her closer.

"God, Avery, you are so damned hot." He kneaded her. "I want to taste every inch of you, but all my cock wants is to be lodged deep inside you."

Heat arrowed between her legs. She leaned down and nipped his lips. "Well, then. Do it. I'm all yours."

***

Roth felt like all his control was pouring off him as steam. Two words pounded in his head: *Mine. Take.* He tugged Avery off the desk and went to work tearing her clothes off.

She tried to help, kicking her trousers and panties away. He pushed her shirt off and ripped her bra away with one hard tug.

Then she was naked in front of him, and his chest tightened. Gorgeous. Fucking gorgeous. She had curves, but they were toned. Sleek muscles were visible in her legs, in her belly.

He sank back in his chair and then tugged her forward into his lap.

She let out a quick expulsion of air, her legs settling on either side of his hips. Damn, never in all the hours of sitting in his tiny office had he ever imagined having a sexy, naked woman in his lap. His cock was so hard it felt like he was going to burst.

Avery leaned forward and her mouth nipped along his neck, making him groan. She licked his skin, her teeth scraping along the tendon in his neck where she'd marked him earlier. Roth's hips surged up.

She nipped him again. "I like sinking my teeth into you."

"I'll make you pay for that."

She shimmied against him, the bare center of her rubbing along his hard cock, separated by just his trousers. Then she bit down on his neck. Hard. He growled. She sucked on his skin, making a small sound in her throat that said she was enjoying the flavor of him.

Roth slid a hand down, delving between her sleek thighs. She was all heat and soft skin. She made another cry, this time throwing her head back. He reared up and clamped his mouth on her exposed neck.

"Roth!"

"Payback," he murmured against her skin. He licked, sucked and nibbled on her until she writhed against him.

He couldn't wait any longer. He pushed her back on his thighs, yanked his shirt over his head and unzipped his trousers. He cursed as he struggled with the awkward position, and when she let out a laugh—a pure, happy laugh—he felt a warmth inside, separate to the molten desire raging through his blood.

He couldn't take the time to get his trousers completely off. He simply freed his cock as best he could.

When he looked up, his heart stopped.

Avery's gaze was glued to his cock. She slipped off his legs and onto her knees, bringing her face right in line with him. Jesus, had he ever seen anything more provocative?

She gripped his cock and made a small sound that he figured was designed to drive a man out of his mind. Then she flicked a hot glance up at him, leaned forward and sucked him in.

He swallowed a curse. His cock had already been hard as hell, but now, with her warm, tight mouth on him, he felt bigger than he'd ever been. "God, sweetheart...that's it, take all of me."

She did, swallowing against him, relaxing her throat and sucking him down. Roth slid a hand into her hair, not to direct her, but because he needed to damn well hold on to something.

Avery pulled back and licked at the underside of his swollen cock, and she seemed to find a place that sent electric tingles racing down his spine. His legs trembled and then she swallowed him again.

He groaned. "Shit..." The only words his incoherent mind could conjure were curses.

She moaned on his cock, sucking harder, the vibrations making him groan again. He felt his impending release growing, coiling at the base of his spine. His hips pushed forward against his control.

"No." He gripped her under the arms and yanked her up. As much as he wanted to spill in her pretty mouth, he wanted to come inside her more.

He pulled her onto his lap again, the chair squeaking like crazy. She fitted her thighs on either side of his hips, and the head of his cock brushed at her hot folds.

She made a humming noise, shifting her hips and the head of him lodged inside her.

"Wait, wait." His fingers dug into her hips to hold her there. Poised above him, her face flushed with desire, her eyes just a little wild.

His control was slipping. He'd prided himself on it...from the moment he'd made the decision to join the Army. His life had been about learning to fight better, about protecting, about never losing control.

But this woman...she challenged him, pushed him, and even here, in this sensual moment between them, she dragged feelings out of him he wasn't ever sure he'd wanted to feel.

She moved her hips, rubbing against his hard cock. "Roth?"

"Do you have a contraceptive implant?" He forced the words out. "I just had mine removed. It was past its use-by date, and the doc is still working on how to replicate new ones." It hadn't been an issue for him, since his sex life had been sporadic.

Avery hovered there, her mouth open. "I have one, but, God, mine would be past the use-by date, as well."

"Wait, wait." He wrapped an arm around her and leaned forward. That made his cock slide into her another inch and they both groaned again. Desperate, Roth yanked a drawer open and pulled out a foil square.

Avery raised a brow. "You keep a condom in your office."

"It was a joke. From Camryn. She was bitching at me that I worked too hard and needed to get laid." Reluctantly, he set Avery back again and tore open the condom. He was really out of practice, but he got it on.

Before he could say anything, Avery was moving back over him. "I need you, Roth." Her voice had turned low and husky. Her hands ran up his arms and settled on his shoulders.

"Take me, sweetheart."

Her gaze drilled into his as she cupped his cock and lined it up between her legs.

Roth felt like he couldn't breathe. Then, she pushed down, taking him inside her.

Chapter Nine

Avery felt the heat pouring off Roth, felt the hard strength of him beneath her and his hard cock parting her.

Her heartbeat, already racing, tripped. He was big, and she hadn't had sex for a long time. He felt enormous inside her.

"Relax." His lips touched just under her ear.

"You're too big." Those clever lips made her shiver. "But I can take you."

"I know you can." His strangled laugh rumbled through his chest. "Damn, you're tight."

She pushed down more, letting him slide deep. She felt his thumb brush her belly, then slide to where they were joined. A second later, he rubbed her clit in a hard, slippery circle.

Avery cried out.

"I'm going to move now," he growled.

"Do it," she panted.

He slammed up, lodging deep inside her the last inch. She gripped his shoulders, biting her lip. She was so full, stretched.

And it felt so good.

He flicked at her clit again. "Avery…ride me."

Yes. She lifted her hips, then slid back down.

She rose and fell again, then looked into Roth's face. His ice-hued eyes were glittering with fierce desire, and the tendons in his neck strained as he watched her riding him.

"So damn good, sweetheart." He kept working her clit. "You're so tight around me, and I can't wait to feel you come on my cock."

His words made her stomach clench. "Roth."

"All that matters right now is you and me," he said.

Him and her. The two of them. Avery's throat thickened. She'd been alone all her life, knew it was best not to let anyone in. But now, with him moving inside her, filling her up, she let herself imagine he was hers. That it was just the two of them. Avery and Roth.

Suddenly his hand slid into her hair, tugging her head back. "Stop thinking," he said on a growl.

He moved, so the angle of his thrusts went just a little deeper. She cried out, feeling a wash of sensation rush through her. Her orgasm, just a shimmer of promise before, moved closer, her body winding tighter.

She saw he was looking down with fierce satisfaction on his face, where his thrusting cock was sliding into her. She looked down, saw the flex of his hard abs and the way his hand was buried between her legs.

"Come for me, Avery." He pressed down harder on her clit, and his other hand tightened in her hair. Blue eyes stayed on hers, watching, waiting, demanding. "Come, dammit."

Avery splintered apart. The fierce pleasure stole her breath, made her scream. She felt herself clamp down on his cock, and then he was groaning. She closed her eyes, the pleasure swamping her.

"Like a fucking vise." His head bowed forward and hit her chest.

Then he surged upwards, lifting her in the air. A second later she felt the cool surface of the desk under her back and heard papers sliding to the floor.

He leaned over her and hammered inside her. Oh, God. She felt her orgasm crest again, and she arched up.

He thrust into her one last time and held himself deep. He groaned and she felt his cock pulse as he filled the condom.

Avery collapsed back. Her muscles were completely lax and she felt the best she had since she'd awoken to the nightmare of the alien invasion.

She wasn't sure how long they stayed there, splayed on the desk, with Roth covering her still-quivering body, but soon she felt the chill of the ventilation on her bare skin.

Roth shifted, and Avery made a small sound.

"Shh, I've got you." He stood, taking her with him into his arms. He set her on her feet and grabbed at her clothes. He helped her into her panties and trousers, his palms running along her skin whenever he encountered it.

"Roth—"

"Shh." He held out her bra and shirt.

While she put them on, he quickly dealt with the condom and yanked on his own clothes. Then he snatched up the maps that had fallen onto the floor, and dumped them on the desk.

"Come on." He grabbed her hand and pulled her out of the office.

Bewildered, Avery had to jog to keep up with his long strides. They hurried out of the Ops Area and down the tunnel to the personal quarters.

Mac strode around a corner and spotted them. "Hey, boss—"

Roth raised a hand and brushed past his second-in-command without a word. Avery glanced back and saw the woman watching them, a wide grin on her face.

When Roth reached his door, he opened it, and pulled her inside.

Then he lifted her up and she squeaked. He dumped her in the center of his bunk and started pulling the clothes he'd just put on back off again.

"Get naked, Avery."

Looming above her, his hard body bare, he took her breath away. Every hard ridge of his abdomen, the broad chest and strong arms. Not to mention that hard, thick cock that had just brought her a lot of pleasure. He was all strength, all man, and she wanted him. She wanted to immerse herself in him and feed the hunger.

He took a second to rummage around in the bedside table and pulled out a long strip of condoms.

Her eyes widened. "Another joke?"

"I plan to use every one of them." He wasted no time sliding one over his hard cock. Then he planted one knee on the bed, yanked her trousers open, and ripped them down her legs. He gripped her ankles and dragged her closer. She gasped. The look on his face warned that anyone who got in the way of what he wanted would regret it.

And Roth Masters wanted her.

Next, he hooked a finger under her panties, and in one hard yank, tore them off her.

"Roth!"

His big hands circled her knees and pushed them wide. He cupped her ass and pulled her up to him. "Again, Avery. Now. All night."

Avery heard the unsaid word *always,* but she knew it was her pleasure-soaked brain imagining things. She knew *always* was just a fantasy.

As he covered her, his cock thrusting inside her, Avery lost the capability to think and all she could do was feel.

***

Late the next morning, Avery opened a locker in the squad room and pulled out the armor inside. She'd never worn this model before, but it was similar to what she'd used at the CCIA. She started fastening the carbon fiber plates over her black cargo pants and shirt.

As she moved, she felt a twinge between her legs, and her thigh muscles ached. She smiled to herself. She was thankful she stayed in shape, because a night with Roth Masters was a hell of a workout.

They'd woken tangled together on his narrow bunk. She pressed her fingers to her swollen lips. She'd rarely spent the night with a lover, partly because work had kept her too busy, and partly because she hadn't thought she'd like it. Sharing her intimate space, trusting someone while she was vulnerable in sleep, wasn't in her nature.

She'd been wrong. She liked it a lot.

Avery heard female voices and a door slammed.

The women of Squad Nine rounded the line of lockers and paused at the sight of her.

Avery nodded, her shoulders tensing slightly, and kept working on the armor. She lifted another panel and saw the deep gouges in it. She fingered them. Raptor claws.

"Sorry about that." A woman with dark hair that glinted with red stepped up beside her, smiling. "That's my old armor. But we're about the same size, so Roth thought it would be the best fit for you. I'm Taylor."

"Avery."

"Oh, we know who you are, Ms. Secret Agent."

Avery glanced past Taylor and saw a tall, Amazonian woman with impossibly long, toned legs lounging on the nearby bench, pulling off her wedge heels. Her black hair was cut ultra-short, accenting her bold cheekbones and striking face. Her skin was smooth and dark, and her gaze was very direct. She crossed her long legs and made no effort to hide the fact she was checking Avery out.

"It's never been a secret I worked for CCIA."

"Ignore Cam." Mackenna Carides stepped forward and thrust out a hand. "She lives to be contrary. We haven't officially met. I'm Mac."

Avery had heard all about Mackenna, and in one glance, Avery knew the woman was tough and no-nonsense.

"Avery." She shook Mac's hand.

Mac's lips quirked. "Welcome to Squad Nine."

The fourth woman had her locker open. She yanked off her civilian clothes, standing there in a sports bra and boy-short panties that highlighted her lush but toned curves. She had dark eyes and long, brown hair that was a mass of curls. She started yanking on some cargo trousers. "I'm Sienna. So, you're the one who has the boss' boxers all in a twist."

Avery's pulse tripped. "Ah...something like that."

Mac eyed her. "He's been telling us he's after whatever knowledge you have about the aliens. We're soldiers, but we're also women...we aren't stupid."

Avery looked at her warily. "Okay."

"Man wants in your panties, Secret Agent," the Amazon said with a wink. "And I'm Camryn, by the way."

Avery nodded. "Not sure we should be discussing Roth's boxers right now." She went back to fastening her armor.

"Well, you have them good and twisted. Man is driving us all insane." Cam's white teeth flashed in a beautiful smile. "You'd do us all a favor if you put him out of his misery and in doing so, put us out of ours."

"Cam, enough," Mac warned.

Cam held up her hands. "Just telling the truth. Besides, my guess is that the boss man would give you a mighty fine ride." Then her gaze sharpened on Avery and her smile widened. "But I think Secret Agent here has already taken the stallion for a spin."

"Oh, ew." This from Taylor. "I feel like we're talking about my brother having sex. Stop it."

"My eyes, my eyes," Sienna cried.

Avery fought a smile. "So...none of you have ever—"

"No!"

"No way."

Cam shook her head violently. "But we know the man is made the way a man should be." She studied Avery's face until Avery wanted to squirm. "Yep, you did the dirty with the boss. Hallelujah."

Avery felt a flush of color in her cheeks and mimicked zipping her lips sealed.

"Roth is important to us." Mac's voice was quiet and her gaze just a little scary. "Just so you know...you hurt him, we'll hurt you."

"And we know a lot of ways to hurt people," Taylor added.

Avery raised a brow. "I was an agent with the CCIA. I bet I know more."

"Hoo...a challenge." Cam winked. "Nice to see you have balls."

"Pretty, girly ones, of course," Sienna added with a smile. "My mother was Italian and said they had a saying in her village—"

The other three women groaned. Cam slapped a palm over her eyes. "Not one of your village sayings."

Sienna ignored her squad mates. "*Le armi delle donne sono la lingua, le unghie e le lacrime.*" She spoke in a beautiful, lyrical lilt. "The weapons of women are words, fingernails and tears." Sienna's smile turned a little mean. "The old men who came up with that one got it really, really wrong when it comes to Squad Nine."

And with that, the interrogation was over.

They all finished dressing. When Avery hooked her combat belt around her waist, Mac stepped forward, holding out a carbine. "Used one?"

"Yes." Avery took it. Checked it. The laser charge pack was showing full. "I preferred a plasma battle rifle, but this will be fine."

"Good. Come on, we need to get to the hangar. We're taking the Darkswifts in."

As they moved through a short tunnel, Avery felt a rush of excitement. Going on a mission. *Finally.* The chance to fight back and be useful.

And on top of that, she was about to get to ride in a Darkswift.

They entered the hangar and her gaze fell on the crafts she'd heard about. Avery felt as though time suddenly slowed. "God, they are gorgeous."

She heard the other women chuckling, but she ignored them and ran her gaze over the sleek, dark lines of the craft. They were built for stealth and speed.

Mac pointed at the first one. "That's your ride. You'll be with Roth."

Avery moved closer and ran her hand over the smooth metal. "I only ever saw prototypes of these babies. I've never flown in one."

"And you won't fly one today." Roth's voice echoed in the hangar as he strode up to them. "Passenger only."

Camryn sniffed. "Men. Can't ever let a woman drive." She gave Avery a side glance. "Does he let a woman drive in bed?"

"Cam, focus on the mission." Roth's gaze drifted down Avery's form, taking in her armor. She barely stopped herself from fidgeting. Did no one else see that hot blaze in his eyes? It made her think of the things they'd done to each other throughout the night. Finally, he nodded. "You ready?"

"Ready."

Roth touched a panel on the side of the Darkswift and the black cockpit screen slid back. There were two body-shaped spaces on the craft. Roth gestured to the left side and Avery stepped up, lying down on her belly. The seat was molded, and she shifted a bit until she got comfortable. The controls sat directly in front of her.

Roth lay down smoothly beside her and started tapping at the controls. Avery glanced over and saw the rest of Squad Nine climbing into their Darkswifts. Mac with Sienna. Taylor with Camryn. Avery frowned. "There should be one more on your team. Who'd I displace for the mission?"

"Theron." Roth smiled. "At six foot five, he was more than happy to stay behind. He finds the Darkswifts a tight fit. He'll be sitting with our comms officer, Arden."

The cockpit screen slid closed, enclosing them in a dark cocoon. A heads-up display flared to life in front of both of them, and Avery studied everything on it.

"Initiating launch," a steady, feminine voice said through the comm line.

Roth touched his ear. "Arden, meet Avery. Avery, Arden...she takes very good care of us while we're in the field."

"Hi," Avery said.

"A pleasure to meet you, Avery. Good luck out there and if you need anything, just let me know."

"Got it." Avery heard a siren and watched the hangar doors slowly open.

"There's a launch mechanism in the floor," Roth said. "It'll shoot us out into the air."

Ahead, Avery saw a beautiful valley stretched out below them. It was covered in a sea of trees, and for a second, the beauty of it caught her and her chest swelled. Since her rescue, she'd been stuck in the base, with only a few nocturnal visits to see Dino. Before that, she'd been locked in a tank in the lab.

She'd almost forgotten that beauty still existed in the world.

She turned her head, her gaze tracing over Roth's rugged profile. He wasn't beautiful by any stretch of the definition, but he was a healthy, attractive male in his prime.

"Launch in sixty seconds," Arden said.

Avery savored the excitement singing through her blood. She listened as Arden counted down to launch, heard the quiet chatter from the rest of Squad Nine.

"Ready?" Roth asked.

She nodded. "Let's do it."

Arden finished her countdown. "Three. Two. One. Launch."

The catapult mechanism released, and sent the Darkswift shooting out of the hangar.

With breathtaking speed, the Darkswift sped into the sky.

Chapter Ten

Exhilaration fizzed in Avery's blood. That anticipation she felt, heading off on a mission—a feeling she'd missed so much. She also felt so...happy. The only other time she'd felt like this, Roth had been kissing her.

Beside her, Roth turned his head and smiled at her. His hands were moving smoothly over the controls. The Darkswift banked to the right, the move making her stomach dip, and she had a fantastic view of the scenery below. She saw some magnificent rocky outcrops at the edge of the mountains. And trees, so many trees. It was stunning.

Moments later, she saw the other two Darkswifts move up on either side of theirs.

"Good hunting, Nine," Arden said. "And be careful."

"We will, Arden," Roth answered.

Through the comm, Avery heard Mac and Taylor answer the woman as well.

"All right, illusion systems up. Let's head south," Roth said. "Keep your eyes peeled. Arden's monitoring the drone feed and will let us know if she spots any alien activity."

Soon, they moved over the outer suburbs of Sydney, and all the thrill of the ride was sucked out of Avery. As signs of the city's awful destruction came into view, she felt like she'd swallowed a stone and it sat heavily in her gut.

God. She saw entire swathes of houses—full neighborhoods—razed to the ground, nothing left but rubble, like a tornado had ripped through. But she knew it had been alien bombs, raptor troops, and rampaging rexes who were responsible for the devastation. In other places, the buildings were just burnt-out shells, surrounded by overgrown grass and vegetation.

She didn't spot a single living thing—human or animal.

Avery pressed her fingers to the cockpit screen, her heart so heavy in her chest. If she'd been smarter, worked harder, done *something* more, maybe she could have prevented this.

"Not your fault, Avery. It's stupid of you to take the weight of this on yourself."

She glanced at him, swallowing to wet her dry throat. He wasn't looking at her. "I was head of the team—"

"Team. Not a single superhero. You represented the Coalition. Besides, no one's at fault." He scowled. "Although Howell needs to be hung up and left for the raptors." Roth stabbed a finger at the devastation below. "Only things to blame for that are the damn raptors who invaded a planet that wasn't theirs."

She nodded, but a part of her wasn't convinced.

Strong fingers wrapped around her arm and she jerked her head back.

Ice-blue eyes blazed. "Avery, they were going to invade, no matter what you did. You have to work the guilt out and move on to beating their scaly asses now." He let out a short breath. "If you keep blaming yourself, that guilt will eat you alive. You have to accept they died and there wasn't anything you could have done."

Those words steadied her. Or maybe it was he who steadied her. His strength, his determination, his solidness. An irresistible combination. She pressed her hand over his. Or maybe it was what she heard buried in his voice. "That's how you felt...about your family?"

"Yeah." He stared straight ahead, lost in his thoughts. "I felt like I'd failed them. I had these dreams for months after they died...that if I'd been with them, I could have saved them." He looked at her again. "I learned to blame the terrorists who killed them."

"And you joined the Army to fight the terrorists."

"Yes. I won't lie. It helped."

And now he was giving her the chance to fight back against the aliens. "How come some pretty young thing back at base hasn't claimed you?"

He grinned. "Pretty young things can't keep up with me." His voice lowered. "And I seem to have a thing for strong women who get off on trying to beat me up."

"You have a team of those."

"But I also like women who have dark hair, beautiful hazel eyes, and fiery, independent dispositions."

Avery opened her mouth to respond, her body tingling, but Arden's urgent voice cut through the line.

"Ptero ship, three klicks to the east. It doesn't have a bead on you, but I suggest you move away from it. Illusion systems will keep you undetectable unless you get too close."

Roth's face turned serious and he tapped the controls. "Got it, Arden. Thanks. Nine, adjust heading away from the ptero."

Avery looked to the east and saw the ptero in the distance. She'd seen the ship that had brought the Gizzida to the meetings—an incredible, fluid design. The ptero was smaller, and looked like the flying dinosaur it had been named for. It had large, fixed wings, sharpening to a pointed cockpit at front, and a long, tail-like back end.

Soon, the ptero slipped out of sight and Avery focused back on the ground below. They moved over green, overgrown farmland, and the remnants of small towns, and ahead, she saw the ocean.

"What are we looking for?" Avery asked.

"Any sign of regular movements. If there are people in a bunker around here, they'd be coming up, maybe for food, or intel, or just to get outside. We might see regular paths or disturbance."

Avery nodded, looking down at the ground.

"The comp's running scans. It'll mark anything interesting."

"Boss?" Mac's voice. "If we spot anything promising, we going down to have a look?"

"Not this trip. We mark it, take the info back to base, and then we'll come back if we have to."

A large escarpment dominated the area. In parts it was sandstone cliffs, and in others, a wide plateau covered in trees. She saw the glint of a large dam. It would have given a beautiful view of the sea.

"The Illawarra Range," Arden informed. "It was a mix of conservation areas and private property owned by the mining companies."

They flew over several mine locations, but since they were underground mines, there wasn't much of interest on the surface, just a few dilapidated buildings.

After twenty minutes of flying, they had a handful of potentials marked, but nothing Avery thought was a shoo-in. She tapped a finger against her seat. Maybe Howell never made it to his bunker? Hell, maybe he never got the bunker made in time. Who knew what had happened while she was locked in that cage?

"Moving onto what was the location of the Saddleback mine," Roth said.

Avery spotted the mine's offices, as well as a coal preparation plant for washing the coal. The steel framework of the plant was still standing, but vegetation was doing its best to overrun it.

There was no sign of life. Nothing that made it stand out.

She eyed the ruins of the prep plant for a long

moment. It took her a second to realize what she was looking at, but when she did, she blinked. "Roth. Take a look at the top of the plant."

He frowned and wheeled the Darkswift around the structure. "Shit...is that an antenna?"

It was well-hidden, made to look like junk. "Looks like it. And it looks like it is in perfect working condition."

"Damn. This could be it."

Avery searched the ground harder. "Look. I think there are some pathways through the grass, but they've stuck to the trees in an effort to hide them."

"Hot damn. Nine, I think this is it. Mac, you have the camera, snap me some pretty pics."

"You got it, bossman."

"Taylor, circle out and see if you can pick anything else up around the edges of the mine property."

"On it," Taylor replied.

His team respected him. Avery wasn't surprised. She'd already guessed he was an excellent leader. "Can you take us in any lower?"

He nodded. "Increases the risk of being spotted, but I think it's worth it. Mac, I'm heading in for a closer look."

The Darkswift dipped and Avery had to swallow back her laugh. God, she loved these things.

Suddenly, Roth pushed them into a hard dive, and when she glanced over at him, he was smiling. She realized he was doing it for her. For the first time in a long time, Avery laughed, hard and loud.

But soon, they were both focused on the ground below.

"Can you see anything else?" he asked.

"No." If Howell and any human survivors were indeed living here, they were being careful to keep themselves hidden.

"Roth." Arden's voice. "The drone is picking up a faint heat signature on the ground. Ten meters southwest of the coal prep plant structure. In what looks like trees."

"We'll check it out." Roth turned the craft.

"There are the trees." Avery pointed to a large, lone stand of trees surrounded by thick bush.

Roth cursed. "If anyone's in there, they're too well-hidden. They picked their spot well."

A flash of something caught Avery's eye. "I think I might have just seen a reflection off binocs." She stared, trying to spot something through the foliage. Her eyes watered from the strain. "Can't see a damn thing."

"We'll mark it and come back with a couple of squads to take a look around."

"Roth." This time it was Mac on the comm. "Sienna and I are headed a little farther west. Thought we might have spotted something there."

"Go," he said. "Avery and I will swing around for another look at the mine, then we'll all rendezvous at the meeting point." He rattled off some coordinates. "After that, we'll head back to base and take a look at everything we've got."

"Got it," Mac said.

Avery stared at the space where she guessed

Mac's Darkswift was hiding, imagined it peeling away. "You really aren't going to let me have a go flying? I've piloted gliders before. They're sort of similar."

"A glider is nothing like a Darkswift. And no, you can't fly until you're qualified."

She poked her tongue out at him.

His eyes darkened. "Careful. I might take that as a challenge."

Avery felt a hot rush flash through her. She liked challenging Roth Masters.

They did another circle of the mine, lower this time. Everything remained quiet and still.

"Roth!" Arden's voice broke through, loud and urgent, and made Avery jerk. "I have some strange heat signatures heading your way. They're airborne."

"What?" Roth arched his neck looking out the cockpit screen. "I don't see anything."

"There are four of them, and they're big. Not pteros, though."

Avery scanned the area as well. She didn't see anything.

Then something slammed into the cockpit.

"Fuck." As the Darkswift veered to the right, Roth grabbed the controls, struggling to get them level. "Illusion system's down."

Another...thing slammed into the cockpit, and Avery grabbed onto the handholds built into the molded seat. She caught a glimpse of a long, black body and...wings.

"It's some sort of flying creature," she called out.

As the animal flew over them, she tried to keep it in sight.

Bam. Another hit. This time the creature didn't fly away, but pulled back, hovering in front of the cockpit screen.

"Oh, my God," she murmured.

"What the hell?" Roth was staring, too.

It was some sort of giant, alien insect. It had a long, elongated body, a head topped with huge, multifaceted eyes, and a large mouth with serrated mandibles on either side. It had two sets of large and strong-looking, transparent wings.

The creature rushed forwardand slammed into the Darkswift. The strength of the hit knocked the craft to the side again.

Another alien insect crashed into them, and another.

"Dammit." Roth was fighting the controls. "We can't get out of here if they keep this up." He rammed down on the throttle.

The Darkswift shot forward, shaking unsteadily as it went, as though it were drunk.

Avery looked to the left and saw one of the alien insects clamped onto the wing...eating it.

"Roth, they're eating the metal on the wing!"

"Arden, we're under attack—" A metallic screech came across the line.

Avery and Roth both winced and wrenched the earpieces out of their ears.

"What happened?" Avery said.

"No idea. But we've lost comms." He was focused on the controls. "Man the laser cannon, we need to get these bastards off us." Icy eyes looked her way. "Or we're going down."

Avery activated the touchscreen, and after Roth gave her authorization, the laser cannon controls flared to life on the heads-up display. She studied it for a second, and was relieved to see it was similar to other weapons' systems she'd used before. "All right, let's go bug hunting."

Roth kept the Darkswift moving. Avery aimed the cannon, ready for the second when an insect got in range. *Come on, you ugly things*. She waited. A flash of golden wings caught her eye, and she fired.

She heard the inhuman screech from outside the cockpit. One giant bug fell back, plummeting to the ground.

"Shit, there's another one on the other wing," Roth said. "Damn things are chomping through the steel like its sugar."

Two on the wings, one down. Where was the other one? Avery waited, her muscles tense, forcing herself to stay alert.

A hard thump on the cockpit. She looked up and saw the fourth insect. It was hammering its head against the synth glass.

Avery banged against the glass. The bug reared back, but didn't fly off.

"Can you shake them off?" she asked.

"I can try. But we're unstable as it is. It's risky."

Above them came a loud crunching noise. She gasped. The glass was cracked like a sheet of ice. "Don't think we have another choice."

Grim-faced, Roth nodded. "Hold on."

The Darkswift pulled hard to the left, its left wing pointing almost vertically to the ground. Avery's stomach dropped.

Roth pulled the craft around hard. One insect slipped off the wing, and Avery lost sight of the creature that had been attacking the cockpit.

"Come on," she cried out. "Get in target range."

"Hang on."

Roth turned the Darkswift hard in the opposite direction. One giant bug pulled into the laser sights.

Avery pulled the trigger.

The insect shuddered, then fell in a death spiral.

"Yeah!" she yelled, smiling. "Two down, two to go."

"And we're almost back to the rendezvous point. We should be in visual range of the others soon."

Backup would be very welcomed. Avery stayed ready.

Suddenly, one of the bugs rushed at them, clamping onto the cockpit. Glass shattered and rained over them in a wild sprinkle of shards. The top of the cockpit was gone.

Avery thought Roth was cursing, but the rush of the wind, combined with the erratic clicking noise the bug was making, drowned it out. The bug reached its head into the cockpit, snapping at her with its sharp mandibles. It didn't have teeth, but she guessed the edges on those things were worse than knives.

Roth was fighting to keep the Darkswift steady.

If they didn't get this bug off, they were going to

crash, or get chomped on.

Grimly, Avery unclipped her harness and grabbed the carbine Mac had given her. She sat up, and jabbed the barrel at the alien.

"Avery!" Roth roared. "Strap in, dammit."

She jammed her knees against the middle console to keep her balance and opened fire.

The green laser cut into the insect's fat belly. Its wings fluttered like crazy, and blood spewed over the craft's wing. The bug slid off, and fell behind them.

"You're crazy." Roth grabbed at her. "Get down here.

She grinned at him, and started to get back in her seat.

The final alien insect slammed into the left wing. The wing, weakened where the other bug had chewed on it, snapped.

The Darkswift tipped down, and Avery fell with the sharp move.

No! Her hands scrabbled for purchase on something—anything. They weren't really that high off the ground, but if she went over, it was still high enough to kill.

She heard Roth roar her name. Her legs fell over the edge of the craft and into open air. She managed to snag something with her hands and held on.

The Darkswift began a nasty spiral toward the ground. She couldn't see Roth, but she figured he was fighting for control. In the dizzying spin and the mad rush of air, she couldn't see much at all.

There was a loud crunch of metal, and a jarring thud.

Then, Avery was flying through the air. Her body crashed into something hard, and pain burst through her in an avalanche.

Everything went black.

Chapter Eleven

Roth woke to a world of pain. He stayed still for a moment, cataloguing the situation. He was slumped over the controls of the Darkswift, his upper body hanging out of the broken cockpit.

He swallowed a groan, trying to remember what had happened. His head throbbed and he felt the wet slide of blood down his face and neck. His body was a mass of aches and pains.

Darkswift. Alien bugs. Crashing. Avery.

Avery. He lifted his head, his heart hammering. The other side of the Darkswift was empty.

God, no. He scrambled up to his knees, heedless of his training warning him to search for the enemy first, find a weapon and take cover.

He had to find Avery.

Roth struggled out of the remains of his harness. He saw his carbine in the holder where he'd stowed it during flight, and snatched it up. Wincing, he stood and jumped out of the broken craft.

They were in a field. There were some trees nearby, but thankfully they hadn't hit them during the crash.

He found his earpiece hanging from its wire and set it back in his ear. He tapped it. While he couldn't contact the base, he prayed he still had short-range contact with Avery. "Avery, you there?" He scanned his surroundings, searching for any sign of her.

Silence.

"Mac? Arden? Anybody receiving." His earpiece was completely dead. Damaged in the crash. He yanked it out and tossed it in the wreckage of the cockpit.

Had Avery climbed out of the Darkswift? Was she hurt? Then more memories cleared in his throbbing head. *She'd been unharnessed.* His chest constricted until every breath hurt.

God. He moved faster, circling the Darkswift, then moving outwards in some semblance of an organized search perimeter. The little idiot had unclipped her harness to fight off the bug. She'd risked her life to save his.

His gut hardened to a tight knot. An image of Avery, broken and lifeless, left him with a cold sweat spreading over his skin.

He kept moving.

He came to a body. But it wasn't slim limbs and dark hair. It was one of the bugs.

Roth nudged it with his carbine. Damn thing was as big as him. It looked like a giant dragonfly with brown-and-gold coloring. This one was definitely dead, its wings a shredded mess.

Then he heard a groan.

Roth whipped his weapon up, eye pressed to the sight.

He saw the creature's body move...then a slim

hand—a very human hand—slid out from under the creature's dead bulk.

"Avery!" Roth dropped to his knees, relief driving into him so hard he could barely breathe. He touched her hand and then gave the bug's carcass a hard shove to get it off her.

Avery looked up at him, her dark hair a mad tangle around her face. "Roth." His name came out a croak.

He yanked her into his arms. "Are you okay?"

"Can't...breathe. Holding me too tight."

He loosened his grip but couldn't let her go. He pushed her hair off her face. "God, baby, I thought I'd lost you."

"Same." She cupped his cheeks. "You're bleeding all over the place."

"Nothing major."

"Good." She rose on her knees and pressed her lips to his.

And Roth forgot all about the crash and his injuries. He pulled her closer and took control of the kiss.

She tasted so good it muddled his mind. He thrust his tongue inside, his cock pushing insistently against his armor. She was alive. He was alive. He'd never felt so good.

When they pulled back, they were both panting.

"When we get somewhere safe, I'm stripping you naked and fucking you hard," he growled.

Avery's tongue came out and touched her bottom lip. "Oh, yeah?"

"Yes. And I'm going to spread those strong, lean

thighs of yours and lick you until you come."

Her breath hitched. "What else?"

"Every damn thing I can come up with. I want to take you from behind and watch my cock sliding into you. I want you laid out under me, legs on my shoulders, so I can watch your face when you come on my cock. And I want to watch you suck my cock again."

With a shaky hand, she pushed at her tangled hair. "Then we'd better get out of this field and find somewhere safe."

Roth took a second to lock his desire down. His body was hungry for her, this woman he wanted beyond reasoning. But another urge was kicking in. He had to get her safe.

He grabbed her hand and together, they stood. "Comms are down and we are a long way from Blue Mountain Base."

She studied the surrounding area, her gaze lingering on the destroyed Darkswift. "Options?"

"I'm going to leave a coded message with the craft. It's likely my squad will find it. I think we need to start moving back toward Blue Mountain."

She gasped. "We're hundreds of kilometers away from base, Roth. It'll take us weeks."

"First things first. I'll leave the message, let them know which direction we're heading. Then we'll take what we can that's useful from the craft."

"Why not stay here?"

"Because every alien in range will know we went down. And if anyone comes looking for these bugs, we'll be sitting ducks. Besides, we need shelter, and

I want to take a look at those ribs you're babying."

She straightened. "Only bruised. I'm fine. I'm damn lucky to be alive. I'm just glad I didn't get tossed out of the Darkswift until we were close to the ground."

Roth felt his muscles harden. "You should never have taken off your harness."

"We'd both be bug chow if I hadn't. Don't go all macho alpha man on me. Come on, we need to strip the craft of anything useful to us."

As she strode over to the Darkswift, Roth scowled at her back. The competent CCIA agent was back.

He followed her, and watched as she knelt on the undamaged wing of the craft, reaching in to pull out equipment. Her position gave him a perfect view of her ass. He closed his eyes. He had to get this under control. They were in hostile territory, and far from base. He needed to focus...and not on Avery's attractive assets.

"Here." A dark-green backpack slapped against his chest. She spun around, holding a small, red first aid kit in her hands. "Let me clean the blood off your face and take a look at that cut."

With a reluctant nod, he sat on the wing. The Darkswift moved a few inches, but settled. Avery pulled out some wipes, knelt, and started wiping his temple and forehead.

She made a humming noise. "A nasty little cut. It'll need some med glue." She kept swiping.

Roth was staring at her chest. She was wearing armor, and he couldn't see anything tantalizing, but he was well aware of what was under the carbon fiber.

She dabbed a little too hard at his cut. "Ow."

She pulled back. "Ow? You're a badass soldier who takes on invading aliens, and this makes you go 'ow'?"

"It stings, smartass."

She went back to cleaning, moving down the side of his neck. "Well, it's clean now. I'll put a bit of med glue on it, and you're done." She leaned over him, gently squeezing the glue into the scrape. It stung for a second, but eased instantly. "There." Then she bent down and pressed a kiss just beside the cut. "All better."

He grabbed her wrist, met her gaze. "Who are you, and where's my ferocious little special agent gone?"

Her smile was crooked. "Guess getting attacked by alien bugs and being tossed out of a crashing aircraft mellows a girl."

"Most people would be freaked out and curled in a ball."

That crooked smile again. "I'm not most people."

He cupped her chin. "No, you're not." He drank in her face, her strong features, and that always-fierce glint in her eyes. "Come on. Sun will set in a few hours and we need to find shelter. Let me leave the coded message and we'll get moving."

***

Avery had enjoyed the walk at first. The fresh air

and the scent of lush grass and green trees had made her feel...fresh, and free.

But now, her backpack straps were digging into her shoulders, and her hip and ribs were aching. No, throbbing—like a sore tooth.

"There's a town a couple of kilometers ahead. We'll be there soon," Roth said.

"I'm fine."

"You're not fine." He grabbed her backpack and pulled her to a halt. "I've asked you three times to give me the pack."

"I can hold my weight, Masters."

"Never said you couldn't." His voice lowered. "I'm not some jerk you need to prove yourself to, Avery." He opened her pack and yanked out the first aid kit, stuffing it into his own.

The lightened pack instantly felt better. "Thanks," she muttered.

He looked like he was fighting a smile. "Gee, that was heartfelt."

She trudged on. "I don't do heartfelt, Masters."

They came to the end of the field and climbed over a sagging fence. A cracked, two-lane highway with a faded white line down the middle stretched out before them.

"All right." She hitched the backpack higher. "Just a couple more kilometers...piece of cake."

Suddenly, green raptor poison sprayed across the road. Avery gasped, just as Roth tackled her. They rolled onto the verge and into the grass. When she sat up, Roth was already on one knee, returning fire with his carbine.

Avery shook her head and snatched up her weapon. Looking down the sights, she saw the raptors, four of them, firing their ugly, scaled weapons that spewed paralyzing poison.

She returned fire. Her focus zoomed in, blocking out the whine of the laser and the buck of the carbine in her hands. The raptors were huge, over six and a half feet, and all muscle. Gray, scaly skin covered their bodies, and their faces were dominated by large jaws and burning-red eyes.

Something inside her trembled, and flashbacks peppered her like shrapnel. Small micro-memories of the lab, of huge raptors dragging her, trapping her in a cage, of pain.

Avery's jaw tightened and she pulled the trigger. Anger was a hot bubble in her chest as she fired at the aliens.

One went down. The others were crouched behind an abandoned car.

"Cover me!" Roth yelled.

What? Avery felt a spike of fear and watched him leap up and sprint toward the raptors. He kept firing, his powerful body moving in a way that was almost graceful.

Almost. There was too much pure power in him to be graceful.

Avery focused back on the raptors. She needed to make sure they didn't hit Roth.

She kept the laser fire focused on them. One ducked back down, another was returning fire, and the third, a really big one, stepped forward to meet Roth.

Roth kept firing, aiming at the alien's relatively unprotected chest. They wore armor-like trousers and boots, but their upper bodies were just tough, scaly skin.

The big one swung out to hit Roth, but he ducked and jammed his carbine under the alien's chin. One shot and the creature fell backward.

Roth planted a boot on the abandoned car, jumped into the air and aimed his carbine down. Avery watched one alien sprint out from cover, trying to escape. Roth kept firing on the other side of the car.

Avery fired at the escaping alien, and he let out some grunts, dodging and slowing down.

Roth landed on the road in a slight crouch, and chased the final retreating alien. As he ran, he swung his carbine onto his back.

Avery swiveled, keeping her weapon aimed. What was he doing?

Another few long strides, and he pulled a large gladius combat knife from his belt. He leapt onto the back of the retreating raptor and took him down.

It was a short, bloody struggle. Sunlight glinted off the long, sturdy blade of the combat knife. She saw no pleasure in Roth's tough face. Just determination. He stood, cleaned his blade on the grass, and strode back toward Avery. She got to her feet.

"You are a badass."

That earned a slight grin from him. "Thanks for the backup."

"Pretty sure you didn't need it."

He shook his head. "Backup is important. Working together is the way we'll beat these guys. They're bigger, they have advanced tech, but we stick together, we look out for each other."

She stared at him for a second. She'd thought he was arrogant, a driven man out to prove how big and bad he was. But he wasn't. From what she could tell, his squad loved him, and he took care of them right back.

He was really just one of the good guys. A man who wanted to protect those who weren't as strong, a man fighting for what was right.

"Come on," Roth said. "These guys won't be alone."

She nodded, and after Roth hitched his backpack on his shoulders, they headed off.

"I think we'll walk through the trees. Raptors don't like them."

They left the road, walking among the trees lining it. "Why?" she asked.

He raised a brow.

"Why don't they like the trees?"

"We aren't sure, but we think there's something the trees give off they don't like. You know Santha Kade, right?"

Avery nodded. "Head of spies."

Roth barked out a short laugh. "She'd love hearing her recon team called spies."

"I've met Devlin Gray."

Roth scowled. "Oh? You've spent time with Gray?"

She recognized that tone. Devlin was a handsome, cultured, former British spy, and Santha's right-hand man. Not that he'd shared his past with anyone at Blue Mountain Base, but Devlin and Avery had run into each other once or twice in their former lives. "We've chatted."

Roth made a skeptical sound and Avery rolled her eyes. "You were saying? About Santha's team?"

"Right. Anyway, while Santha was holed up in the city fighting the aliens all by herself—" there was admiration in his voice "—she discovered that the alien canids hate cedar oil. We've created some cedar-oil grenades since then, and they are a great deterrent."

Canids were the ugly alien hunting dogs she'd heard about, but never seen. "In the negotiation meetings, they mentioned their planet is volcanic and rocky. Didn't sound like there was much vegetation, let alone trees."

He stared at her for a second. "That's good intel. Make sure you pass it on to Santha when we get back."

If they got back. Avery looked up at the sky. The sun was just starting to turn the western horizon orange. Darkness was coming, and so far, there'd been no sign of Squad Nine's other Darkswifts in the sky.

A big hand grabbed hers, long, strong fingers twining with her own. She looked up, and the tightness she hadn't realized had crept into her chest eased. She wasn't alone. She and Roth were together. They'd get through this.

They kept walking, and soon they passed a few abandoned houses. They were almost at the town.

Then a chilling sound in the distance made them both pause.

Howls.

"Shit. Canids." Roth looked at her. "Run."

They broke into a stumbling run. The grass was long, tangling around their knees.

The excited yips and howls got closer. Avery fervently wished they had some of those cedar-oil grenades.

"Fuck, they've got our scent," Roth muttered.

They were being hunted.

Chapter Twelve

"Onto the road," Roth barked. "We'll be able to move faster. There's no point being in cover. The canids can sniff us out."

Avery raced up the small embankment and onto the pavement. She glanced behind them, and her heart stopped.

The pack of creatures was loping toward them. They were large—larger than regular dogs—with a row of sharp spikes along their backs. Their glowing red eyes and mouths full of sharp teeth were the stuff of nightmares.

"Avery!"

Roth's shout made her whip around and start running.

She pumped her arms and legs, running as fast as she could, until her lungs were burning.

They rounded a curve in the road. The canids were gaining. They were so damned fast.

The town appeared ahead—or what was left of the town. Some houses were dilapidated or burnt out, just black piles of rubble. Others looked in perfect condition, except for broken windows and overgrown yards.

Roth and Avery sprinted into the town. "We need to find somewhere to hole up. Preferably somewhere high."

Right. "Maybe a roof?"

But most were sagging or missing. They bolted down what she guessed had been the main street. Long-abandoned shops had been looted or boarded up months ago.

At the end of the street, they spotted something that made them both skid to a halt.

"What the hell?"

The street was blocked off by a huge wall of rubble and junk that rose at least ten meters above them. It consisted of old cars, sheets of metal, chunks of concrete, old refrigerators—apparently whatever the residents had been able to get their hands on.

Avery swiveled and saw the canids sprint into view.

"Shit." She spun back. "We'll have to go around it."

They both knew the canids would be on them by then.

"We can try and climb it?" Roth suggested.

Avery could tell it was too unstable. They'd slide right back down, or get swallowed by the junk.

A low growl made them step closer together and turn.

A huge canid slunk forward on its belly. Its mouth was open, showing off those wicked teeth. Drool slobbered from its jaws.

Avery and Roth whipped their weapons up.

The rest of the pack moved in behind the creature.

The lead canid leapt. Avery and Roth fired, but even under the barrage of laser fire, the creature kept coming.

"Fuck." Roth dropped his carbine and pulled out his knife.

But the canid's gaze was fixed on Avery. It pounced. Her heart pumping, Avery kept firing, saw green laser tearing into alien flesh.

The beast slammed into her. She felt the sting of claws on her side, smelled rotting meat on its breath. Roth rammed into the creature and she saw him stabbing it with his knife.

The canid's vicious jaws snapped inches from Avery's face. She turned her head, and tried to heave it off her.

Then it let out a squeal, and Roth shoved it away. It fell into the dirt beside them, dead.

Chest heaving, she sat up.

"You okay?" He wasn't looking at her. His gaze was on the rest of the pack. He helped her get to her feet.

The remaining canids were growling and pacing, a few beasts crouching, ready to attack.

Avery swallowed and stepped closer to Roth. Her side was burning, but she could walk, that was the main thing. "I'm fine."

They couldn't hold them all off. Not with two laser carbines.

"Hey," a voice called from above.

Shocked, Avery glanced up and saw a small,

metal ball fall from the sky. It hit the ground in front of them.

As she watched, the ball sprouted legs and tottered toward the canid pack. She frowned. What the hell was it?

"Hey, you. In here."

Avery spun with a gasp. A gap had opened up in the junk wall and a boy's head popped out. He looked about twelve, his dark hair in need of a cut.

"Quick." He gestured them toward him. "Get in."

Avery shared a brief glance with Roth, then dived through the door. Roth shouldered in behind her.

The boy reached around and slammed the door closed.

There was a loud boom on the other side, and the entire junk wall rattled. A tin can fell down, clattering and rolling onto the ground nearby.

"Jesus." Roth rolled to his feet. "Well, we're alive."

Avery stood, surprised to find herself a bit shaky. She looked at the boy. "Thanks to you."

The boy shrugged a shoulder. "Getting eaten by alien dogs wouldn't be much fun."

She smiled. "No. I imagine not." The memory of foul breath and sharp teeth flashed in her head.

The boy was wearing clean clothes and running shoes that looked brand new. His face glowed with health and he looked well fed. "Hi. I'm Bastian."

"Hi there, Bastian." Avery smiled and took in their surroundings. She saw that the fortified junk wall circled a group of about six houses, and what looked like a grocery store.

Roth held out a hand to the boy. "Thanks for the save. We wouldn't have made it without your help."

Bastian blinked, then subtly his chest puffed up. He took Roth's hand and shook it. "So, you're military?" He was eyeing their armor and weapons.

"Yes." Roth nodded.

"You're really a soldier? Not just a regular person turned fighter?"

"Career soldier. Special Forces."

"Wow. Have you killed lots of aliens?"

Avery watched Roth smother a smile. They shared a glance. Yep, kids always seemed interested in the same things.

"Yeah, I have," Roth answered. "So many I've lost count."

Avery limped forward. "Our aircraft crashed near here."

"Aircraft?" the boy asked, wide-eyed.

"It's called a Darkswift. A two person craft and glider."

His eyes opened more. "I saw you! I saw three shimmers in the distance."

Roth nodded. "The rest of my squad. We lost contact when alien...bugs attacked us."

"The giant dragonflies." Bastian's nose wrinkled. "They breed around here, and they are always hungry. They'll eat anything."

"We haven't seen them before," Roth added. "We're from Blue Mountain Base."

The boy gasped. "The secret underground base in the mountains?"

"Yes."

"But…that's just a fairytale."

"I assure you, the base exists," Avery said. "It's home to hundreds of people." She looked around. "We have running water, electricity, food. Bastian, do you live here?"

"Oh, no. People used to live here, but they've been gone a long time."

"Are your parents here?" she asked.

His smile evaporated, and he looked at the ground. "My parents are gone."

Avery's heart clenched. She knew that look. God, she'd worn it herself during her childhood. "I'm sorry."

She really wanted to touch him, but she'd hated that, as well. Kind, well-meaning strangers touching her, sympathy in their eyes. Then they'd leave and go back to their cozy lives and families.

"Do you live alone?"

He shook his head and Avery took another step toward him, but this time, electric pain shot through her side and she cried out. Her leg went out from under her, and she saw the dirt rising to meet her.

Roth caught her. "Avery?"

"Something hurts," she panted through the pain.

Roth patted her side and she cried out. He pulled his hand back and Avery saw the blood. A muscle ticked in his jaw, his eyes hardening. "Canid got through your armor."

***

Roth laid Avery on the ground, hating when he saw her wince. He shrugged off his backpack and looked at Bastian.

"Bastian, can you fish around in there and pull out the first aid kit?"

The boy knelt, nodding furiously.

Roth set to work pulling Avery's armor off her side.

"Sorry," she muttered.

"Nothing to be sorry for." With her armor off, he lifted her shirt and winced. "Damn, sweetheart. That has to hurt like hell."

"Just a little. I didn't feel it at first."

Roth turned and Bastian held out the first aid kit. "Thanks, kid."

With a nod, Bastian scuttled backward. "She'll be okay?"

"Yeah." Roth would make sure of it.

The boy nodded. "I'll check the wall. Make sure no more dogs are hanging around."

"Be careful," Avery said.

"I always am." Bastian scurried away.

Roth ripped the kit open, rummaged through, and pulled out the remaining sterile pads. He wiped the blood away. The canid claw had gouged her smooth skin, but it wasn't as deep as he'd feared. He smeared some med gel on—it would ease the pain, and stop any infection. Not to mention speed up the healing a little.

He pressed an adhesive over the wound.

"How's that feel?"

She smiled at him. "Better."

He let his fingers brush gently over her bare stomach. "Wish I was shoving your clothes out of the way for a different reason than this."

Her smile was wide. "That makes two of us."

He dipped a finger in her belly button. "When we get back to base…"

She gasped. "Yeah, you told me."

He helped her up, glad to see the color back in her face.

"What's your take on Bastian?" she asked.

"Resourceful," he said. "Lonely."

She nodded thoughtfully. "But well cared for." She glanced at the empty houses. "He isn't living here."

"No, he isn't. And we need to know where he's from."

Moments later, Bastian reappeared. "No sign of the dogs." He looked at Avery. "You're okay?"

She gave a nod. "Roth fixed me right up."

The boy's shoulders relaxed. "Good."

Roth looked around again. It was time to get some answers. "Hey, Bastian, I wanted to ask—"

Shouts suddenly echoed around them. Roth lifted his carbine and saw a group of armored soldiers running at them.

"Drop the weapons!"

"Get down on the ground!"

There were twelve of them. Roth's hands flexed on his weapon. "I'm Colonel Roth Masters of—"

"On the ground," a woman roared. She rushed up and grabbed Bastian. She yanked him backward and shoved him at a soldier behind her.

She was in charge, Roth decided. The woman looked like she was in her early forties, her dark hair in a chin-length bob under her helmet. She held her carbine like she knew exactly how to use it.

The soldiers surrounded them, all stony-faced. Roth took note of them all, and their pristine armor and well-maintained weapons. No raptor claw marks or dents to be seen.

"We don't mean any harm," Avery said. "Bastian saved us from some alien canids—"

"I'm not going to say it again," the woman said, her voice hard. "Drop your weapons and get on the ground."

"Listen—" Avery began again "—we just want—"

Something whizzed through the air and slapped into Avery's armor. *What the hell?* Roth stepped in front of her and saw her eyes widen.

He saw the small device's prongs had dug into her unarmored chest. Dammit. A shockround. A second later, her body started shaking as the high-voltage ran through her.

Roth grabbed her. He saw soldiers converging and he fired his carbine one handed, taking down the soldiers nearest to them.

Then he felt a shockround slam into his shoulder. As the electric shock hit him, he managed to roll so he hit the ground first, Avery on top of him.

He saw the grim face of the woman in charge above him. He struggled to stay conscious, gritting his teeth and trying to keep his hold on Avery.

Then he saw the butt of a gun descend and everything went black.

Chapter Thirteen

Avery groaned and struggled to sit up. Her muscles were aching like she'd spent hours in the gym.

She blinked, then went still as her brain recognized her surroundings as unfamiliar. Where the hell was she?

Then she remembered. She scrambled to her feet, a hand pressed to her chest where she'd been hit with the shockround. Her armor and weapon were gone, and she was in a cell. There were three concrete walls and one that was just metal bars.

She strode to the bars, staring into the empty hall. More cells lined the corridor. Where was Roth? Her throat tightened. Was he okay?

She forced herself to calm down and assess the situation. She was in a locked cell. There were no windows, just a row of muted lights built into the top of the wall, and she heard the steady whoosh of the ventilation, so she guessed they were underground.

Avery paced across the small space. The contents of her cell consisted of a narrow bunk and a built-in bench, and that was it.

A low groan made her freeze. She raced to the bars, trying to see into the cell beside hers. "Roth?"

"Avery." His voice was low and raspy. A second later, he appeared at the bars.

She couldn't see him that well, but she slipped a hand through the bars and when his strong fingers wrapped around hers, she released a breath. "You're not hurt?"

"Ache like hell, but I'm fine. Damn shockrounds. You?"

"I'm good." She tried to see his face, and when he shifted, the dim light illuminated his black and swollen right eye. She gasped. "They beat you!"

"Gun butt to the face. It'll be fine. Nothing's broken."

Avery's other hand tightened on the bars. The assholes. They'd seen that Avery and Roth hadn't meant any harm but they'd still stormed in like they had something to prove. "This is Howell's bunker, isn't it?"

"That's my guess." Roth fiddled in his pocket and withdrew something tiny.

Avery frowned, pressing her cheek to the bars to see. "What is that? An insect?"

"It's a mini-drone. Noah designed it. I tested one in the alien ship on a previous mission." He touched it and the little drone took to the air, flitting there like a bug, before it zoomed away. "It'll take a look around and send info back to my mini-tablet."

"They left you with your tablet?"

He smiled. "Not my well-hidden, backup one. It's tucked into the sole of my boot."

"Well, aren't you a boy scout?"

He stroked her palm. "Not always."

Footsteps echoed in the hall. Avery sucked in a breath and Roth squeezed her fingers. "Showtime."

Two people appeared in front of them. The woman was the leader of the soldiers who'd brought them in. Her face was set in the hard lines of someone used to command. The man was an opposite story. Avery made note of his stats: six foot, broad shoulders, green eyes and long, dark hair that he had tied back at the base of his neck. He had a compelling face, strong and brooding. Unlike the woman, who wore fatigues, this man wore well-worn jeans and a T-shirt. Both of which were splattered with streaks of paint. Actually, he had paint on his hands as well.

"Who are you?" the woman demanded.

"You could have asked that question before you shot us with shockrounds," Avery suggested.

The man looked at the woman with a raised brow.

The woman straightened. "I'm Captain Kate Scott. I run security here. Since we're in the middle of a hostile invasion, we don't tend to chit-chat with strangers."

Avery gripped the bars tighter. "Do either of us look like damned aliens? We're on the same side."

Captain Scott's mouth tightened.

"Avery." Roth's tone held a hint of warning.

The man stepped forward. "I'm sorry if the captain was overzealous in her duties. But believe me, she holds the safety of our residents as her highest priority. I'm Nikolai Ivanov. And whether I like it or not, I run the civilian side of things in the Enclave."

"I'm Colonel Roth Masters. We're from Blue Mountain Base."

"There is no Blue Mountain Base," the captain said.

"Since I've been based there since the invasion, along with about a thousand other survivors, I respectfully disagree," Roth said. "I'm also head of one of the squads fighting the aliens under General Adam Holmes."

The captain's eyes widened. "You're *fighting* the aliens?"

"Of course." There was a frown in Roth's voice. "What else do we do with them?"

"Avoid them," the captain replied.

The paint-splattered man was looking at Avery. "And you? You're part of the colonel's squad?"

"Not usually, no. I'm Avery Stillman. I was with Coalition Central Intelligence." Hot anger filled her throat. "And I'm guessing you're both part of the elitist group of assholes put together by Howell, who sold out humanity."

The captain's eyes narrowed and the man frowned and cocked his head. "I have no idea what you're talking about. The Enclave was specially designed to house survivors of the alien attack. People were selected at random by government officials. We have men, women, children. Professors, historians, artists—" he held up his hands ruefully "—scientists, and more. We are the hope for the continuation of humanity."

Avery's face twisted. "I'm guessing Howell sold you that bullshit."

"President Howell set up this place, yes." Nikolai shoved his hands in his pockets. "He's the third leader of the Enclave."

"Howell is scum," Avery spat. Memories of her time with the aliens flashed through her head. "I was part of Howell's negotiation team with the aliens. He sold us out. In return for his own safety and this precious place—" she waved a hand around "—he let them destroy the world. To take human prisoners. And he damn well gave me to them."

"Sydney is in ruins," Roth said quietly. "Our squads have destroyed numerous alien labs and testing facilities. Billions of humans are dead. And those who are left are scrambling to survive."

Both Kate and Nikolai looked stunned.

Nikolai finally cursed under his breath in what Avery guessed was Russian. That seemed to shake the captain out of her spell. "We don't know you. Howell has only done good things by the people of this Enclave. He deserves a chance to tell us his side of the story." The woman straightened. "I'm sure there's been some misunderstanding."

Avery wanted to scream. She felt Roth's gaze on her, warning her to be quiet.

"Kate, open the cells," Nikolai said.

"What?" the captain said, frowning.

"It's dinnertime. Let's bring our guests to the dining room, and let them see what our Enclave is like."

The captain looked like she wanted to protest, but finally pulled out a master key and opened the cells.

"Roth needs a doctor to look at his eye," Avery said, moving to his side.

"And Avery has hurt ribs and a canid injury."

The captain nodded. "I'll see that a technician takes a look at you both. I never meant for you to be injured...you took down four of my people while under the effect of the shockround, so we had to subdue you."

Roth nodded. "It's fine."

"No, it's not," Avery muttered.

Roth squeezed her arm.

"Come on," Nikolai said, leading the way.

They left the spartan prison cells and moved into a hall. Avery gasped. This was nothing like Blue Mountain Base. The tunnels were laid with thick, sumptuous carpet, and gorgeous paintings lined the walls.

"These are beautiful," Avery said.

Nikolai smiled. He couldn't quite be called handsome, but his smile made him incredibly attractive. "These are from an art gallery, brought here to be kept safe. We also have a thriving artists' community here at the Enclave."

"You're a painter?"

"I paint, but sculpting is my primary medium." His gaze ran over her face. "I'd love to sculpt your face."

Roth edged closer. "I don't think so."

Nikolai's smile widened and he inclined his head.

Avery took quick glances into some of the rooms they passed. One was filled with high-tech comps, another was a huge games room; one even contained a huge, indoor swimming pool.

They passed some people, who smiled and called out hello. They all eyed Avery and Roth curiously. Everyone looked happy, healthy, and well-fed.

The light was different, too. Avery stared up at the warm glow of the lights. In Blue Mountain Base, the harsh, fluorescent lighting could get a bit much. But here, the light was more muted, nicer somehow.

"We have a sunlight system."

She glanced up and saw Nikolai looking at her. "Sorry?"

"An experimental sunlight system. It mimics real sunlight. It's much healthier for the residents."

"And this is all built in a coal mine, right?"

"That's right."

Captain Scott wrinkled her nose. "How did you know where to find us? What gave us away?"

"Avery saw Howell's plans, that's why he sold her out," Roth said. "She knew his bunker was south of Sydney somewhere."

"And we saw the antenna on the old coal prep plant when we flew over to take a look," Avery added.

"Dammit." The captain frowned. "I told my team it needed to be better hidden." She released a breath. "We take security very seriously. The aliens don't know the location of the Enclave, and President Howell ensured there are no plans or schematics of the place to fall into enemy hands."

"I bet he did," Avery said drily.

The captain's mouth tightened. "Here's the health center."

The health center was a large well-stocked and well-staffed space. Avery took in the high-tech equipment and shelves packed with supplies. She watched as Roth was checked over. Her own doctor checked her ribs and told her what she already knew—nothing broken—refreshed her bandage on the canid scratch, and gave her a painkiller.

"Dinner awaits," Nikolai said with a smile. A short walk from the health center, they reached large arched doors. "Here's the dining room."

They stepped into the large room. It had high, arched ceilings, and a collection of tables that made it look like a restaurant, all set with snowy-white tablecloths, beautiful patterned china, and lovely silverware.

Avery's throat tightened. It looked like the residents of the Enclave did everything in luxury.

However, the dining room was empty.

A woman in her twenties bustled out of the kitchen and came to an abrupt stop. "Oh." She shot Nikolai a flirtatious look before her gaze settled on Roth, her eyes going wide. "Visitors."

"Angelina," Nikolai said with an edge of frustration. "Where is everyone?"

"Oh, President Howell decided we should have a picnic. Everyone's up in the Garden."

"Thanks," Nikolai said. "Come on."

He led them down another hall, and soon they walked into a room filled with narrow, long, open vehicles with two-person carriages behind them.

"Hop in." Captain Scott held open the door to one carriage.

Avery climbed in, and Roth sat beside her. With Roth's broad shoulders, it was a tight fit. He shifted and put his arm around her.

She leaned into him. God, she had to admit it was nice to lean on someone. To have someone beside you when everything had gone to hell.

Just don't get used to it, Avery.

The captain sat in the driver's seat, Nikolai beside her, and the vehicle moved off.

Ahead, doors opened and they drove into a dark tunnel.

Here were signs of the tunnels' true origins. Rough walls, pipes strung along the roof, patches of coal.

Soon, the tunnel started to ascend. Next, they reached a spiral ramp, and the engine on the vehicle droned as it carried them upward.

Roth leaned down, his lips brushing her ear. "I think we're going up the inside of the escarpment."

Soon, the ramp ended, and they drove down another flat tunnel, then through a door, and they were once again in a well-lit parking area, filled with similar vehicles.

They stopped and their hosts got out.

"Come on," Nikolai said. "We'll find President Howell in here."

They walked through another set of doors, and inside, Roth and Avery froze. Her mouth fell open, her gaze traveling upward. "Oh, my God."

"Damn," Roth muttered.

"Impressive, isn't it?" Nikolai was grinning. "We call it the Garden."

They were in a bowl that had been cut into the escarpment. Rock walls rose on either side, and above, the night sky glittered with a sprinkle of stars. In the garden, a crowd of people sat on picnic blankets and outdoor chairs on the lush grass. Everyone was munching on food, chatting and laughing. Kids were running around, chasing each other.

To one side was a large, fenced garden area with healthy, thriving vegetables in neat rows. Old Man Hamish would go into convulsions of joy over it. To the other side were trees and flowers. The trees were strung with fairy lights that gave the place a surreal fairyland feel and, in places, Avery spotted hammocks strung between the trees.

"How do you protect this?" Roth asked.

"We have an illusion system that keeps it hidden," Nikolai said. "From above, this just looks like any other patch of trees on the escarpment."

"We do have doors we can close in an emergency, too," Captain Scott added.

"What about the alien bugs?" Avery asked.

"They don't come up here to the top of the escarpment," the captain answered.

Roth shook his head. "Still, if the aliens find this, the entire Enclave is compromised."

"Like we said before, we work hard to keep our location a secret," Nikolai said. "And we also have a lock-down system."

Avery frowned. "Lock-down system?"

It was Captain Scott who answered. "If the aliens find any of the entrances to the Enclave, we have a high-tech security system that kicks in. A series of metal security doors slam down, and they are all protected with high-voltage electrical fields. We then can pull all residents back to the central core."

Roth nodded thoughtfully. "Like a panic room."

"Exactly. We have two years' worth of supplies in storage and the ability to produce everything we need if we are locked in."

Avery still wasn't sure how she'd feel about being trapped with the enemy knocking on the door. The sound of kids squealing with laughter caught her ear, and she looked up to see an amazing treehouse perched among the branches, with several children riding a spiral slide back to the ground.

This place was beautiful, and yet horrifying all at the same time. Here, these children were having fun, completely insulated from the horrors above. Yet, the adults had to know. These people were hiding out here, pretending that nightmarish atrocities weren't happening to the rest of their fellow humans above.

Then she spotted Bastian. The boy caught her attention and lifted a hand in greeting. Okay, maybe not all the children were insulated. In

Bastian's face, she'd read pain and grief. So the Enclave wasn't all hearts and rainbows.

"Ah, President Howell, good evening." Captain Scott's voice broke through Avery's thoughts. "We have some people who need to talk with you, sir."

"Newcomers?" The man once in charge of the entire Coalition came toward them. He wore dark slacks and a blue shirt. He had a face perfect for a politician—clean-cut, a square jaw, a wide smile. The public had loved it. And while everything had been running well, he'd been an excellent leader.

Until the aliens had arrived. When the going got tough, he'd crumpled and shown his true colors.

He opened his arms, smiling. "Welcome to the Enclave."

Avery stepped forward, and she had the intense pleasure of watching him stumble to a halt. His face blanched.

She'd thought she'd known what she was going to say to him. How she'd act. But everything she'd seen, the pain and terror she'd felt in the alien lab, the helplessness of lost memories, not to mention the fact she'd almost ended up being turned into an alien while this man sat here in luxury, crashed in on her. "You fucking asshole."

Avery launched at him. She took him down, slamming her fists into his head.

Arms wrapped around her and lifted her off Howell. She kicked and struggled, but Roth held her against his chest. "Easy."

But she couldn't let it go. She stared down at Howell, who was still sprawled on the floor. "They put me in a tank, asshole. They tried to turn me into a goddamn alien...and they've done it to millions of other people. The blame's on you, Howell. All those lives, they're on you."

"Easy." Roth turned her to face him.

She felt her lips tremble. God, everyone had turned to watch the drama and she didn't want anyone to see her pain. As a child, she'd hidden under her bedcovers to cry. She'd never let anyone see.

"I've got you." Roth pressed her face into his chest.

She gripped his shirt and held on. She cried silently, her tears soaking his shirt.

His lips pressed against her hair. "I've got you, Avery. Always."

Chapter Fourteen

Holding onto Avery was the only thing stopping Roth from going after Howell himself. One little twist, and it would be so easy to end the bastard who'd hurt her.

She always showed everyone her strength, so the silent tears he felt on his skin almost broke him.

Howell was spluttering as Scott helped him up. A pretty, slender blonde woman hurried over, two small boys hovering beside her. Roth recognized Howell's young wife and family.

"President Howell, do you know this woman?" Captain Scott asked.

Howell tugged on his shirt, straightening his mussed clothes. "Agent Stillman is clearly traumatized by whatever terrible circumstances she's endured. Last time I saw her, she was...upset that she hadn't been selected for the Enclave."

Avery whipped around, that familiar glint in her eyes. She took a step forward and two soldiers moved in front of Howell.

Avery didn't make a sound. She kicked one in the knee and he toppled. She turned and slammed a fist into the other man's face. Something broke in his nose and blood gushed. She was moving again, landing a hard kick at the man struggling to get back on his feet. Roth winced, but didn't move. He knew just how hard her blows were.

Besides, he figured these dickheads deserved it.

A perfectly executed front kick sent the man with the broken nose crashing into a chair. She turned to Howell.

But Roth knew he needed to stop this before Scott's soldiers hurt her or dragged her off to a cell. He grabbed her, pulling her to his side and looked at Howell. "You want to say that again?"

Roth's low, lethal tone made Howell take an automatic step back.

"Daddy, did you give that lady to the aliens?" one of Howell's sons, a boy of about five, asked.

Howell's mouth opened, then closed.

Roth saw Captain Scott squeeze her eyes closed and nearby, Nikolai cursed under his breath.

"Gregory, what is going on?" Howell's wife demanded.

"Mrs. Howell, because of your husband, most of the Coalition's citizens are dead." Avery glared at Howell. "I don't know what lies you've been telling these people, but there are survivors out there." She pointed upward. "Some still hiding in the ruins, some running from the aliens, and the rest of us are finding ways to fight back."

"We have a lot of innocent people over at Blue Mountain Base," Roth added, sliding his arm across Avery's shoulders. "Survivors of the alien labs, children, military personnel who go out there every day to fight. But we recently found out, Howell, that you sold all the Coalition military information to the aliens in return for them leaving you and your Enclave alone."

Gasps echoed around. A muscle ticked in Howell's tight jaw.

"That means our base is no longer safe. There's every chance we'll have to evacuate. That's why we came here. To investigate your secret bunker, and see if it was a viable alternative for our people."

Howell dragged in a deep breath, found his composure, and put on his best politician's smile. "Like I said, Agent Stillman is traumatized. Whatever she's told you, it isn't true. And I'm sorry, but I can't jeopardize the lives of the people here by overcrowding the Enclave with more survivors."

"Or you don't want to sully your artists, scientists, and beautiful people," Avery spat. "Or more importantly, don't want to risk your own hide and comfort."

"Enough." Captain Scott stepped forward. "Sir, I think you, Nikolai and I need to have a meeting."

Nikolai made a sound and his gaze hit Roth's. He looked pissed as hell. "We absolutely need to have a meeting. The three of us are in charge here, remember, not just you, Howell."

Oh, Roth would have liked to have been in on that meeting.

"But first," Nikolai said, "I think our guests need to be shown to their quarters."

"You mean our cells," Avery said.

"No." The artist's voice was firm. "Kate, have one of your people show Roth and Avery to one of the guest rooms."

The captain hesitated, then nodded and waved one of her security team over.

Roth ushered Avery out of the Garden with one last, scathing glance at Howell. He kept his arm around her as the young soldier showed them to a vehicle and drove them back to the main part of the Enclave.

He felt Avery vibrating with anger. The tears were gone, and his ferocious agent was back.

After a short walk from the vehicle, the young man opened a door. "Here's your room." He waved them in.

The room was quite spacious, and Roth eyed the large bed. After eighteen months of squeezing his large frame into the narrow bunks at Blue Mountain Base, the double looked huge and beyond inviting.

"Bathroom's through there." The man glanced at them both. "Ah, I believe you'll find some basic medical supplies under the sink."

"Thanks," Roth said with a nod. He caught a glimpse of a large bathtub. Jesus, a tub. He'd never been a bath man, but when you no longer had a choice—because baths at Blue Mountain Base were a rarity—you suddenly missed what you didn't have.

"Ah, and the captain's ordered someone to be on duty out in the hall. To ensure your security."

Avery made a small sound and Roth squeezed her arm. Yeah, they both knew the guard wasn't for their security. "Thank you."

As soon as the soldier was gone, Roth moved to the door and opened the electronic door lock panel. "Avery, can you reprogram the door lock to only work for us?"

A muscle ticked in her jaw, but she nodded and set to work. Roth pulled his mini-tablet from his boot and pulled up the data from the mini-drone. He looked at Avery and paused. She had her tongue between her teeth as she worked. It was kind of cute.

He looked back at his screen and tapped in some commands. "Okay, I have the drone coming back to our area. If anyone other than a single guard enters the corridor out there, an alarm will sound."

Avery set the panel back on the lock controls. "Done. No one can open this door but us."

"Good work."

"Roth, we have to get out of here."

"I know."

"I don't trust Howell."

Nor did Roth. He touched her hair, tucking a strand back behind her ear. "We'll get out."

"You have a plan?"

He sank onto the bed. "Not yet. I really, really wish I could contact my squad."

She started pacing. "We could sneak out, knock our guard out, and search for a comms room."

"The place is huge, Avery. Unless the drone's picked something up, we could spend the next week looking around, searching for comms devices."

"Then we focus on getting out. Howell can't risk keeping us alive and jeopardizing his cushy existence."

Roth wanted to hold her close and take away her pain. "I know." His hands curled into fists. "I can kill him for you, before we leave."

"Roth." She closed the distance and stepped in front of him. "Howell has stolen enough from me." She cupped Roth's cheek. "No more."

He grabbed her around the waist and pulled her in between his legs. He pressed his face to her belly. "No more."

The door chimed and they pulled apart. What now? With a scowl, Roth strode over and touched the panel. "What?"

"You have a visitor," the guard said.

With a glance at Avery, Roth opened the door.

And saw Bastian standing there.

***

"Bastian?" Avery said.

He shot them a lopsided grin. "Hi."

"Five minutes, B," the guard said. "Then you need to be gone."

The boy nodded. As the door closed, Bastian studied Avery. "You look mad."

She huffed out a breath. "Yeah, I am."

He shoved his hands in the pockets of his jeans. "Mr. Howell...he really did what you said? Gave you to the aliens?"

"Yes. He did."

That same, sad look from earlier crossed Bastian's face. "My parents. They lived here, too. They spoke out against Mr. Howell. They said we should be fighting the aliens, not hiding."

Oh, no. "What happened to your parents, Bastian?"

"Mr. Howell banished them." A ragged whisper. "That's why I go out. I hope I might find them."

Avery closed her eyes. How many others had been banished? She'd thought Scott and Ivanov seemed genuine, but maybe they were just Howell's lackeys. When she opened her eyes, she stared at the young boy.

He was so young. He should have been safe with his family, going to school, playing. Damn the Gizzida and Howell. "That isn't safe, Bastian."

The boy's jaw firmed. "I'm good at it."

She sighed. Yeah, she guessed he was. The aliens had stolen so much, and that clearly included the innocence of children like Bastian.

"I brought something for you." Bastian managed a shy smile. He held out a small, clear packet filled with pale-pink grains. "Bath salts. You were injured, and these are supposed to help. Some of the people here make them."

Avery took the package. "Thank you, Bastian. This is just about the best gift I could have received today." She smiled. "There are no bathtubs at our base, so I'll enjoy using these."

A flush again. "You're welcome."

Roth crossed his arms over his chest, and leaned

against the wall. "Bastian, you know we aren't staying, right?"

Bastian's smile evaporated and his feet shifted restlessly. "Yeah. Maybe...maybe I could come with you?"

Avery straightened, and saw Roth do the same.

"You have friends here. It's the safest place you could be," Roth said.

"What if my parents are at your base?"

Avery's heart broke. God. There was so much longing and hope in those words.

Roth took a deep breath. "I can check for you. But you can't get your hopes up, okay?"

"Okay."

"Damn." Roth raked a hand through his hair. "I wish I could get in contact with my team."

"I...uh—"

Avery and Roth both pinned the boy with their gazes. "What is it, Bastian?" she asked.

"I have a radio. I made it."

Roth went still, just staring at the boy.

"You made a radio," Avery said.

He nodded. "I've never used it to contact anyone, but sometimes I pick up voices."

"Can we see it, Bastian?" Roth asked.

Another nod. "But—" the boy's voice trailed off.

Feeling protective, Avery stepped closer. "It's okay, Bastian."

"I made the radio myself. Most of it's from junk...but I had to, uh...borrow a few parts from storage. Mr. Howell doesn't know." Bastian fidgeted. "He'd be mad."

"We won't be sharing with him, kid," Roth said. "Anything at all."

"Okay." Bastian reached for the bag slung over his shoulder. He paused again. "You'll really check?"

"Yes." Roth touched Bastian's shoulder. "I promise."

Watching Roth with Bastian made some of Avery's earlier anger flare. Howell was selfish scum, nothing at all compared to a true hero like Roth.

"If you want to come to the base, we'll take you," Avery said.

Roth frowned. "Avery—"

"We'll take care of him, Roth. Here, they sent his parents away and left him an orphan. He deserves better."

"I know that. But our base isn't safe anymore."

Bastian considered. "There's good food there?"

"Yes. I work with the chef, so I can guarantee that." Avery wanted to hug him, but she'd been a child alone. She knew he wouldn't accept it. "And there's a school, as well. And an awesome tech team who make all kinds of gadgets like your radio and that little insect bomb you designed."

"A tech team," he breathed.

A heavy sensation formed in Avery's belly. She reminded herself that the base wasn't safe. Was it the right thing to do, to take Bastian from this place, where he was at least alive, to somewhere that could get him killed?

Bastian reached into his bag and rummaged

around. He pulled out a small, but bulky, radio made of a mishmash of parts.

Roth took the device. "Holy hell, kid. Noah—the grumpy guy who runs our tech team—would recruit you in a second."

Avery watched Bastian help Roth adjust it and explained the tiny flat screen panel and the controls.

"Blue Mountain Base, are you there?" Frowning, Roth adjusted it again. "Blue Mountain Base. Arden? You on the comm?"

Avery held her breath and stared at the small radio. All they heard was a mocking silence.

"This is Masters. Anyone there?"

He kept trying, but when he cursed under his breath, Avery's shoulders slumped. She touched Bastian's shoulder. "It was worth a try. Thank you."

"Roth!"

The scratchy voice exploded through the radio, and all three of them started.

"Roth, oh my God. Are you okay?"

Roth lifted the radio. "Mac?"

"I'm here. Jesus, we found the wreckage of the Darkswift. We thought you were dead."

"Sorry, Carides. I'm still breathing." Roth released a breath. "It is good to hear your voice. You and the squad made it back to base okay?"

"We did. We searched for you guys as long as we could. Avery okay?"

"Yeah. She's here with me."

"Where are you?" Mac demanded.

"Avery and I made it to a nearby town. Then we ran into soldiers from Howell's bunker. He calls it the Enclave."

"Jesus," Mac said.

"Mac, it's in the Saddleback mine. I confirm, it's in the mine."

"Roger that." There was an expulsion of breath. "Damn, I'm glad you didn't end up raptor bait."

"Me too," Roth said. "Although the Enclave soldiers are of the shoot first, ask questions later variety."

Mac cursed. "Well, you're alive. I wouldn't have wanted to break in a new squad leader."

Avery watched Roth smile. "Yeah, yeah, Carides."

"I'll come out and get you—"

"Night's too risky. We're safe for now."

"Tomorrow morning, then. I'll probably have to stop Camryn from hijacking a Hawk."

"You tell Cam I'll ground her for the next three missions if she disobeys orders," Roth said, his voice firm. "Mac, there are these damn giant alien bugs. That's what brought our Darkswift down."

"We saw the bodies." Mac's distaste came through loud and clear.

"When you come in tomorrow, you keep an eye out for them. And Mac...bring an extra squad. We don't trust Howell at all."

"Got it," the female soldier said, voice grim. "Sit tight, Roth. I'll be there in a Hawk tomorrow."

"Out." Roth ended the connection. He handed the radio back to Bastian. "You're a superstar. You keep this." Roth crouched so he was eye-level with the boy. "Avery and I will leave tomorrow. If you want to come, we'll take you."

Bastian gave an eager nod.

Avery couldn't resist any longer, and ruffled Bastian's dark hair. "Thanks for your help."

The flush in Bastian's cheeks darkened. He backed toward the door. "I'll be going now. Sleep well." The door clicked shut behind him.

Roth wandered over and locked the door. Avery's bad mood crashed back in on her. She wanted to be pummeling Howell with her fists. Emotions clogged her throat. She needed some privacy, to get herself under control again.

Without looking at Roth, she headed for the bathroom. "I'm taking a bath."

She slammed the door behind her.

Chapter Fifteen

Avery flicked on the taps and watched as steaming water started to fill the tub. God, so many emotions were storming through her, choking her. She wrapped her arms around her middle. She felt like she was a little girl again, struggling inside, and trying to make sure no one saw it.

Behind her, the door swung open and Roth stalked into the bathroom. She stiffened. He walked past her, close enough that he brushed against her arm. He sat on the closed toilet seat and stretched his long legs out in front of him, crossing them at the ankles.

"You really think I'm going to leave you alone in here?"

"I'm pissed, Roth." She dumped Bastian's salts in the swirling water. "I'm so angry at Howell and this place, I can barely breathe. I'm really not very good company."

She watched as he started pulling off his boots.

"I think you're hiding from me," he said. "I can see you're upset, and that's okay, Avery."

But he'd told her he liked her strength, her fierceness. She didn't feel strong or fierce right now.

Then he unbuttoned his shirt and shrugged it off, leaving him in a T-shirt that stretched over his broad chest.

When Avery realized she was drinking him in like a thirsty woman in a desert, she sucked in a breath and spun. She started stripping off her clothes. She pretended she was back in the unisex locker room at the Agency. She'd stripped down to her underwear in front of people a hundred times. This was no different.

As she bent and let her trousers slide down her legs, out of the corner of her eye, she saw him watching her. His entire focus was on her, like he couldn't look away.

Okay, maybe it was different. This man had fucked her every way possible, but more than that, he seemed to see straight through to the parts of her she wanted to keep hidden.

She straightened and deliberately slowed down. She undid her buttons. One, two, three. Now she turned and saw his glittering gaze, the stark lines of his face, that intense concentration zoomed in on her. She finished slipping the buttons out of their holes, and her shirt hung loose. She knew he could see her black bra and panties.

He drew in a sharp breath, his gaze traveling downward. When he looked up again, his gaze colliding with her eyes, she froze. Molten. Something hot and hungry was alive in his blue eyes.

Avery felt everything in her contract, and a hot pulse throbbed between her legs. She shrugged her shirt off her shoulders and it slithered to the floor.

His gaze moved down her body again. "Is this my punishment?"

She reached behind her back and opened her bra. "For what?" she asked silkily.

His eyes flickered. "For stopping you from beating Howell to a pulp."

She let the bra drop, enjoyed his hiss of breath. She hooked her fingers on either side of her panties and skimmed them down her legs. "Oh, you mean for your macho alpha shit?"

He was staring at her now. She walked the few steps to the tub, putting as much swing into her hips as she could. It was easy. Knowing Roth was watching her with that intense gaze made her feel sexy.

"I was protecting you."

She stepped into the tub. She knew he was right, but her emotions weren't rational. She'd had Howell right there, under her fists and she'd wanted to hurt him. She sank into the water and didn't quite manage to swallow her moan. The water was fantastic. It lapped around her aching body, and she decided it was a hundred times better than the quick showers she was still getting used to.

Avery finger-combed her tangled hair and let it fall around her. Then she looked up...and gasped.

Roth closed the distance and knelt beside the tub. He leaned in, his face close to hers. "The security team would have hurt you, locked you up, or worse, killed you. I was protecting you, and I'd do it again in a heartbeat."

"I can protect myself," she bit out.

"I know that. But we're on these guys' home turf, and there are more of them than us. Does my protection change the fact that you're capable as hell?"

Avery stilled, just her hand moving through the water. No, it didn't. She'd been so incensed by the very sight of Howell that she wasn't thinking straight. Some of her tension eased. "Roth."

He reached out, fingering the ends of her hair where it fell into the water. His rough calluses brushed over her collarbone, and she shivered.

"If anyone lays a finger on you, I'll end them."

The dark promise in his voice made her belly tighten. It was a fierce declaration...and a promise.

Her gaze wandered over his face, and what she saw scared her a little. He was telling the truth. He would go out there and kill to protect her, even at the expense of his own life. That was what scared her.

She leaned forward and kissed him.

He cupped her cheeks and his tongue pressed against her lips, demanding entrance. She let him in, her tongue sliding along his. He groaned, the kiss turning wild. She clasped his large biceps, feeling the incredible strength of him in those hard muscles.

Suddenly he stood and then climbed into the tub, clothes and all. Water sloshed on the floor and she gasped through a smile. "Roth."

He yanked her forward so she fell against his

chest. His big body surrounded her.

"Told you that when we got somewhere safe, I was going to fuck you."

The slow simmer of desire turned hot in a flash. She licked her lips. "This is safe?"

"Door's locked. The mini-drone is in position. Wish I had my carbine, but I've got my secondary combat knife that I had hidden." He nodded toward the sink and she saw the knife he must have set there before.

He straightened his legs as much as he could and pulled her forward until she straddled him. God, there was something sexy about being naked in the arms of a man who was fully clothed.

As she adjusted her legs either side of his hips, she felt the hard press of a bulge between her legs. They both groaned.

Who was she kidding? She needed him right now. She needed someone to hold on to, and the only one she wanted to hold was Roth. She slammed her mouth to his and kissed him.

***

"Clothes," Avery gasped.

Roth reluctantly pulled away from Avery and stood. He ripped his shirt off.

"Roth, hurry up."

He finished shucking his clothes, and they hit the floor with a wet plop. But his gaze was on Avery.

His pulse was hammering in his head. She was

leaning over the edge of the tub, baring her back to him and looking back over her shoulder. Her wet hair was slicked back against her skull and there was heat in her eyes.

He'd never seen a sight more tempting or welcoming.

Free of his clothes, his rock-hard erection bobbed in front of him. The vision of thrusting into her, seeing the smooth curves of her ass shove back to meet him, made the muscles in his body stretch tight.

He knelt, shaping his hands over her ass, then he gripped her hips. "You want my cock, sweetheart?"

"Yes," she hissed.

His thighs bumped against the back of hers and he slid one hand up her spine to cup her shoulder. "You want me to pound into you until you forget, until the anger is gone and all you feel is me?"

She shoved back against him, and his cock rubbed into the crack between her cheeks. Hell, he'd never been this hard, the veins thick, and everything throbbing for release.

With his other hand, he dipped his fingers between her legs. He groaned. "You're so wet for me." He thrust his fingers into her. He wanted to make sure she was ready. This would be hard and fast, but he didn't want to hurt her.

"Roth, if you don't shove your cock inside me I'll get really angry. When I get angry, I get mean—"

He'd noticed. "Easy." He circled his cock and then rubbed it through her lips. The head slipped into her and she moaned.

Then he froze.

"Roth," she pleaded.

"No condom."

She went still. "What?"

"I don't have a condom. I don't take them on missions." *Hell.*

She looked back at him and they stared at each other. Roth had never had sex without the barrier of a condom or his implant before. He quivered. Fuck, he was a primitive asshole, but the thought of sinking his bare cock inside Avery, of coming inside her, made him even harder.

Her eyes darkened. "You like the idea?"

"I'm healthy. And I love the idea of seeing my come leaking out of you. But...bringing a child into this world..."

She nodded, her gaze clouded. "I know." She paused. "I'm healthy, too." She shifted back and it made him sink about an inch inside her.

They both groaned.

Roth felt sweat beading on his brow. "Shit, Avery. We have to both agree to this risk...it's fucking crazy, but I want you more than anything."

Her face was flushed, her chest hitching with her fast breaths. "Yes. If there's a child..."

"We'll do it together. We'll protect our child, no matter what." He gripped her chin. "It'll be loved."

Her lips trembled then, firmed. "I want you."

His fingers bit into her hips. "You're sure, sweetheart? God, you have to be sure."

She shoved back again, harder this time, and he

slid half way in. He leaned down, his chest pressed to her back and fused his mouth to hers.

Then he pulled back, kept one hand on her shoulder to hold her in place, while the other dug into her hip. He slid all the way out of her tight heat, then slammed home.

Avery cried out, her hands gripping the edge of the tub. "Roth, don't stop. Please don't—"

He'd give her everything she ever wanted, if only she'd let him.

Roth worked himself inside her, plunging into her to the hilt. She was tight and wet, and he was excruciatingly aware that there was no barrier between them—latex, chemical, or otherwise. Her sobs of need drove him on, and when he felt her release explode through her, her body clamping down on him, he threw his head back, gripped her hips and slammed into her over and over.

His release hit him like a crashing vehicle and he roared her name as he came. His hot come spilled inside her and nothing had ever felt quite so right.

He collapsed on top of her and noted she was sprawled limply over the side of the tub. Slowly, he pulled out of her, loving that small, sad sound she made as he slipped out. He pulled her into the tub, cleaned them both, then lifted her into his arms.

"Tired," she mumbled.

"Yeah." He felt the edge of exhaustion riding him too. It had been a hell of a day.

Roth didn't bother to dry them off. He headed for the bed, yanked the covers back and laid her down.

He quickly checked his mini-tablet and saw the drone hadn't picked up anything interesting outside their room. He set it beside the bed, then crawled in beside her and curled around her body.

A sense of rightness stole over him and he relaxed against her. He tucked his face into the side of her neck and breathed her in. He hadn't felt like this since his family had been alive.

"I'm falling in love with you, Avery." He felt her stiffen and his heart tightened. "You don't have to say anything back. Just wanted you to know."

It took a while, but slowly, her tense body relaxed. He clamped down on the need to demand how she felt about him. He knew her childhood had left her wary of caring, of loving, but he was going to damn well show her how good they were together.

For now, he focused on the fact that with Avery in his arms, the rest of the world just melted away. He didn't feel the press of responsibility, or the driving need to be fighting. He just felt good.

"Just sleep now, sweetheart," he murmured and let sleep drag him under.

Chapter Sixteen

A hand shaking her shoulder woke Avery from a deep sleep.

"Avery, wake up."

The urgent tone of Roth's voice had her sitting upright and blinking. "What is it?"

He flicked on the bedside lamp. "The alarm."

It was then she heard it. An insistent *meep meep meep* from Roth's tablet.

"The drone's picked up a group of people headed our way. Get dressed." He was already standing beside the bed, pulling his clothes on. He gestured and she saw her clothes tossed on the bed.

She jumped up and hurriedly shoved her legs in her trousers. "How many?"

"Five."

She pulled her shirt over her head. "Maybe they want to talk?"

"At three-thirty in the morning?"

Right. She shoved her feet into her boots. She saw Roth shove his tablet into a slot on the sole of his boot, and then he tucked his combat knife into the back of his trousers.

The door made a low beeping sound. Someone was trying to get in.

She and Roth moved close together in the center of the room. He touched her cheek and she looked at him. His lips descended, a brief kiss that left her wanting more.

"Follow my lead," he said quietly.

She nodded. Just then, the door lock panel exploded in a shower of sparks.

The door opened.

Gregory Howell strode in, flanked by two guards on either side. They were all stone-faced military types—three men and a woman. None were Scott, which Avery found interesting.

"Come with us," Howell said. He was wearing jeans and a hooded sweater. As they moved into the hall, he flicked the hood up.

Avery saw their young guard sprawled on the floor, unconscious, his head bleeding from a wound. She swallowed. She didn't think Howell was planning a midnight picnic.

"I take it you can't handle your people learning that you aren't the wise, benevolent leader," Avery said. "You're just selfish, cowardly scum."

Howell spun around, his face twisting. "I had a family to protect."

Avery stared at him. In that moment, she felt sorry for him. Fear was written all over his face. He'd been tested, and he'd failed. They said the tough times brought out your true colors. She wasn't sure she believed it, but she figured there was some truth in it. Howell had to live with the fact that under the gloss, he had little substance. That he was no role model to his kids.

"No, you had millions of families to protect. And you failed them." Avery sighed. "No one expected you to be perfect and beat the aliens off singlehandedly. But we expected you to try."

"Just shut up." He spun back around. "Come on."

They were herded into an industrial elevator. As the doors on the cage were slammed closed, one of the guards touched the controls. The cage jolted and started upwards.

At the top, Howell strode out of the elevator and then opened a set of double doors that led into a tunnel. This tunnel didn't look as well-maintained as the rest of the Enclave. One of the narrow, open vehicles was parked ahead with two carriages attached.

The guards prodded Avery and Roth to get in.

They drove down the tunnel, no one speaking. The tunnel was mostly flat and they drove for a very long time, the dark walls whizzing past. Was Howell going to toss them in an old mine shaft?

Finally, the tunnel started to rise, and without warning, they came out an exit and into a coal prep plant. She saw straight away it wasn't the plant near the Enclave. This one was even more decrepit, part of having collapsed.

"Out," one guard said.

Avery and Roth climbed out. They weaved their way through the old, rusting equipment and conveyors, then stepped out into the early morning darkness. The air was crisp and the stars were still bright in the sky.

"What now, Howell?" Roth asked. "You planning

to kill us?"

"No." Something crossed the politician's face before his mouth firmed. "I'm using you as bargaining chips and securing the safety of the people I've vowed to protect."

Avery's belly tightened. "What are you talking about?"

Right then, red lights zoomed overhead. She heard Roth curse.

Two raptor pteros.

Now she realized why Howell had driven them so far from the Enclave. "You're doing it again?" Avery shook her head, shocked. "You aren't protecting those people in the Enclave, you're protecting yourself!" She faced the guards. "What has he said to you to convince you to fucking hand us over to the aliens? We're on the same side! We're all human."

The guards all looked nervous, their gazes flicking from Avery and Roth to the raptor pteros landing in the field ahead of them.

"We should be working together to fight the raptors, not fighting each other," Avery said.

"We're safe at the Enclave. Our families are safe," one guard said. "If we don't help…"

When the man trailed off, realization hit Avery. "If you don't help, then he'll banish you like he's banished others. Follow his crazed orders or you're out."

Howell made an enraged sound and leapt forward. He backhanded Avery in the face. "Shut up!"

Pain exploded, and she sensed Roth moving. But her anger was back, and she was done being Howell's favorite chew toy. She kicked out, catching Howell in the belly. He slammed backward into the ground.

In the distance, Avery heard the familiar sound of the aliens' grunt-like language, and the hairs on her neck rose.

Roth pressed up against her back. "I'm here. We're together."

She closed her eyes. She wasn't alone, and she couldn't find the words to tell him how much that meant to her. Whatever they faced, they'd face it together.

Roth's lips brushed her ear. "I'm not letting them take you, sweetheart."

She reached for his hand. "I think I'm falling in love with you, too."

He jerked against her. "Avery—"

She squeezed his hand and gave a small laugh. "You should know that it scares me far more than those raptors heading our way."

"Sweetheart, I've seen how ferocious you can be. I've no doubt you'll work out this love stuff."

Together, they turned and saw a group of raptors moving closer, their weapons clutched in their scaly hands. The aliens' eyes glowed red in the darkness.

Oh, God. She couldn't go back to one of those tanks. And there was no way she'd let them put Roth in one.

A plan. They needed a plan. "Roth?"

"Just wait, Avery. It'll be okay."

Okay? She frowned. They had no weapons, and were caught between a group of humans who were handing them over to the enemy and bloodthirsty aliens. She realized Roth's body was completely relaxed.

"You have a plan," she whispered.

"I've always got a plan."

In that instant, three Hawk quadcopters dropped their illusions and appeared above them.

And all hell broke loose.

***

Roth watched the lead Hawk swing around and fire on the pteros.

The alien ships exploded in balls of flames.

The raptors on the ground scrambled, swinging their weapons up, but the other Hawks were already moving. One turned and moved upwards with breathtaking agility, allowing the sniper on board to fire on the raptors.

It had to be Finn flying. The man was the best Hawk pilot in the entire base, and could push the quadcopters to their limits in ways the other pilots couldn't achieve.

Roth launched himself at the nearest guard, snatching the man's weapon. The guard stared at him, and then the firefight behind them, with wide eyes. Then he spun and scrambled back toward the plant and dived into cover. Howell and the rest of his guards followed suit.

Roth spotted raptors running toward him and Avery. He lifted the laser pistol and fired. It was no carbine, but the alien he'd targeted dodged out of the way.

"Avery?" When she turned, he tossed her the pistol. Then he yanked his knife out. "Cover me."

"Dammit, no, Roth."

He ran at the incoming aliens. He wasn't letting them anywhere near Avery. He clenched his jaw. He wasn't wearing his armor, which meant he wasn't protected, and he didn't have the built-in exoskeleton that gave him added strength and speed. He changed his grip on the knife. It didn't matter if the raptors were bigger and stronger, he was more dangerous.

Because he had more to fight for.

He slammed into the lead alien. He heard the bastard grunt, trying to get his poisonous weapon around. Roth jammed the knife between the alien's ribs.

Laser fire whizzed past and into the other raptors. Damn, Avery was a good shot. She needed to be on the squads.

Roth stabbed at the raptor, working the knife through the creature's thick skin. It made a keening noise that grated, but Roth kept at it until the alien slumped down, dead.

A huge body slammed into him, lifting Roth off the ground. His shoulder blades hit the dirt, and pain radiated through him.

Right in his face, another raptor grinned, its eyes burning demonic red.

Roth whipped the knife around, but the alien grabbed his wrist in impossibly strong claws. The sharp claws cut into Roth's skin, and as the alien exerted pressure to turn the knife away from its chest, Roth winced at the pain.

He pushed and tried with all his strength to shove the blade into the raptor.

But soon the knife was turned around, the blade aimed at Roth's chest.

Shit. He strained, every muscle in his body aching. The tip of the blade pricked his chest, right above his rapidly beating heart.

The raptor grunted.

"Fuck you," Roth bit out.

The blade slid into his flesh and he gritted his teeth. It burned like hell.

"No!" A slim body leapt over the top of him and slammed into the raptor, toppling it off Roth.

He scrambled up to see Avery straddling the creature's chest, the pistol jammed under its jaw as she pulled the trigger.

Panting, he looked up and saw four raptors circling them. *Dammit.*

Then, like wraiths, shadows slipped out of the darkness. Green laser fire lit up the morning.

Roth watched Mac, Taylor and Cam mow down the raptors.

He heard loud human shouts, and swiveled. Hell Squad was running toward them from the opposite direction, taking down the last of the raptors.

He smiled. Hiding might keep you safe, but fighting back was a hell of a lot more satisfying.

Roth helped Avery to her feet. She was watching Hell Squad and Squad Nine make short work of the raptors.

"Holy cow, remind me not to piss any of these guys off," she said.

"You're okay?" He touched her face.

She smiled. "You know what? I think I am."

"Hey, boss?" Mac swaggered up, holding her carbine. "Next time you and Avery take on a group of raptor soldiers, I suggest you do it with armor on, and more than a puny knife and laser pistol."

Roth clapped Mac on the back. "I'll take that advice on board, Carides. Nice to see you. Good timing."

Mac grinned in the darkness. "As always."

"Marcus," Roth said, nodding at the head of Hell Squad.

"Roth, heard you decided to take a little vacation." Marcus raised a brow. "Thought we'd horn in."

Roth snorted. The rest of Hell Squad stood behind their leader. "Don't recommend it. The service turned out to be pretty shitty."

"You really crashed your Darkswift?" Shaw asked. "That is badass, Masters."

"The giant alien bugs sort of helped. Again, I don't recommend it."

"I thought you were coming at daylight," Avery said.

Roth tugged her to his side, pleased when she leaned into him.

"Nah, the boss included a few code words when I

spoke to him," Mac said. "Asked us to come a little early."

Avery looked up at Roth. "You suspected Howell would try something like this?"

"Yes. I knew he couldn't be trusted." Roth looked over her head. "Speak of the devil."

Sienna was herding the guards ahead of her, jabbing them with her carbine. Theron was carrying a struggling Howell by the hood of his sweater.

"Hi, boss." Sienna smiled sweetly. "Got a present for you."

"Thanks, Sienna." He motioned for Theron to put Howell down.

Running footsteps sounded from behind them. Roth, Avery, his squad, and Hell Squad all turned, carbines aimed.

Captain Scott, her soldiers and Nikolai all skidded to a shocked halt. Their gazes went to the tough soldiers facing off with them, then to the bodies of the raptors and the burning pteros.

"We found your guard," Captain Scott said, clutching her weapon. "We managed to track you through the tunnels."

Roth subtly angled his body in front of Avery. "Captain, tell your team to lower their weapons."

"Scott, take them out!" Howell yelled. "Help me."

The sunlight was just starting to brighten the eastern horizon, so it was easy to see the tension in Scott's face. She ignored Howell, her gaze running over the Hell Squad and Squad Nine members.

Marcus shifted his carbine and stepped forward.

"Look, I got pulled out of a warm bed, filled with my warm woman, to come and rescue Masters from you guys." His voice sounded like gravel. "A pissing match isn't going to make me feel any happier." He lifted his carbine an inch. "Want me to prove to you that my gun's bigger?"

His soldiers moved, Hell Squad flanking their leader. Each looked as badass as the next. Roth watched with pride as his squad members joined them.

Captain Scott's hand gripped her weapon. Her team kept their weapons aimed.

Marcus touched his ear. "Say again, Elle."

Mac was doing the same. "Shit. Arden says she's picking up something."

Suddenly, someone yelled, "Alien bugs!"

Chapter Seventeen

Avery swiveled and aimed her laser pistol. Instantly, she saw the swarm of giant bugs descending on them.

"There are more of them," someone shouted.

She turned her head and saw another dark, moving cloud in the sky.

Roth stepped closer to her and on the other side, Mac moved in. The others from Nine, Hell Squad, and the Enclave soldiers all moved together.

"Aim for the wings," Roth roared. "Let's take them down."

"Hell Squad, ready to go to hell?" Marcus yelled.

"Hell, yeah," Hell Squad answered. "The devil needs an ass-kicking."

Carbines opened fire. Avery blocked everything else out of her mind, and focused on the aliens. They flittered and dodged the weapons' fire. One got through, and slammed into the female soldier from Hell Squad. She went down shouting, and Avery saw two of her squad members leap onto the bug to yank it off her.

Avery kept firing and the bug she was aiming at wobbled and fell from the sky.

Bug bodies were dropping, littering the ground with their corpses.

But for every dozen they killed, one managed to get through.

One insect had sunk its mandibles into Captain Scott's uniform, and was dragging the woman across the ground. She was slamming her boot into its face, but it was tenaciously holding on.

"Kate!" Nikolai yelled.

Roth shouldered one of the Enclave soldiers out of the way. He yanked out his knife, leapt over a dead bug, and landed right beside Scott and the alien.

Avery's heart hammered. She knelt, focusing her fire on anything trying to get to Roth.

He plunged the knife into the bug, two, three times. It gave an ear-splitting squeal and released the captain.

Roth grabbed her by the back of her armor and dragged her back to their group.

"Help! Help me."

Avery turned...and saw Howell in the grip of a bug.

It was flapping its wings, its sharp mandibles clamped around his midsection.

She hesitated. He'd done terrible things, to her, to others.

But the faces of his boys flashed through her head. Bastian's face, and his lonely pain of being without his parents. Her own face, living without family. Howell might be crap, but his boys didn't deserve to suffer. Avery would have taken a drug-addict mother over no mother anytime.

She marched forward, firing at the bug. It jerked, twisting in the air. Howell was kicking his arms and legs, trying to twist loose.

She got close enough to reach out one hand. "Howell!"

He gripped her fingers. She grabbed on and aimed around him to fire at the bug's huge, faceted eyes. She kept her finger on the trigger. Then the gun clicked impotently, and the laser cut off. The charge was depleted.

"No." She tugged on Howell's hand, trying to pull him free.

But the bug recovered, and with a flap of his wings, it rose.

Taking Howell with it.

Howell didn't make a sound. His wide, terrified eyes met Avery's, and his mouth opened with a silent scream. His fingers slipped through hers.

She tried to hold on, but with a hard yank, the bug flew free with its prey.

"No," Avery cried.

Arms wrapped around her. She leaned into Roth and watched the bug fly off with Howell, a few of its fellow survivors following right behind.

"I couldn't just let it take him," she said, her voice thick. "I tried. For those boys inside, I tried."

Roth ran a hand over her hair. "I know, sweetheart. I know."

The quadcopters appeared, hovering in the sky above them. The Enclave members collectively gasped.

"That's our ride," Roth said.

Avery wanted nothing more than a hot shower, and to fall into bed and curl up in Roth's arms. Oh, and to sleep for about twelve hours straight.

Nikolai and Captain Scott stepped forward.

"Thank you," Nikolai said. "After what Howell just tried to do, you could have killed us and left the others for the aliens."

"Not my style, Ivanov," Roth said. "Not that I'm that cut up about Howell. We really came here to see if we could join forces. This is who we should be fighting." He kicked the body of an alien bug. "Not each other."

"If your base is no longer viable," Captain Scott said, her dark eyes glittering, "you come here."

"Kate—" Nikolai began.

"No more debates and discussions, Niko. Howell's gone. We've been questioning everything he's told us, everything he's done, for a long time now." She straightened, her gaze meeting Roth's and Avery's. "I never agreed with Howell, but I tried to do my job. I've always had the best interests of the Enclave's residents at heart. If the residents of Blue Mountain Base need a home, then the Enclave is open to them."

Roth held out a hand. "Thank you. I think if we pool our people and our resources, we can make things safer for everybody."

The captain shook his hand. "And if you need more soldiers, I have no doubt most of my team would be eager to be a part of your war on the aliens." She shifted her rifle. "I'll be first in line."

Avery watched Roth smile.

"We always need good people," Roth said. "And Hell Squad here needs a little competition to keep them on their toes."

From nearby, Shaw made a scoffing noise. "Dream on, Masters."

"Shaw, maybe you and I should have a little challenge in the gym when we get back?" Mac called out.

Shaw rolled his eyes. "Like hell, Mac. You come down to the weapons range and we'll have a shooting match. But no way am I letting you beat me up on the mats. You have a black belt in badass. I don't need a black eye and broken ribs to believe it."

"We should arrange a secure comms line between our bases," Roth said to Captain Scott. "So we can stay in touch."

"Let's do it."

Avery turned to Nikolai. "Bastian...he helped us contact our team. He wants to come to Blue Mountain Base."

Nikolai sighed. "After what Howell did to Evelyn and Hugo...I don't really blame him. I'll have him brought out here. I think that's safer than your quadcopters landing right on top of the Enclave." He hesitated. "I'd like to talk with him first."

Avery still wasn't sure taking him with them was the right thing to do, but they'd promised.

Sometime later, the boy rushed out of the plant, his hair disheveled. He had a bulging backpack slung over his shoulder. Nikolai gripped his shoulders and the two had a quick, intense talk. Finally, Nikolai nodded and stepped back.

Bastian jogged over. "I'm coming."

Roth nodded. "Sienna, can you take care of our guest, please?"

The female soldier stepped forward. "Hey, Bastian. Ever ridden in a quadcopter?" She held out a hand.

The young boy took her hand and followed her.

Roth brushed at Avery's hair. "Let's go home."

Home. Avery held on tight to him, and nodded. She'd always imagined home to be this imaginary place—a cute house, with a fence and a dog in the yard. Somewhere warm and cozy and inviting. Now, with Roth, she realized home wasn't a place.

For her, home had become the man in her arms.

***

Noah

Noah Kim sat on the edge of his desk and tapped his comp screen. He studied the base monitoring system and saw red lights blinking. Hell, the ventilation system was playing up again. He scowled. More problems to fix.

The rest of his tech team were already out working on jobs, so he'd have to sort this one out himself.

His comp pinged and he answered the incoming message. "Kim."

"Hi, Noah, it's Elle. Squad Six and Squad Nine

are on their way back."

"They find Roth and Avery?"

"Yes. Everyone's okay. Apparently they're bringing a young boy back with them. Roth thinks he'll give you a run for your money in the tech department." There was a smile in her voice.

Noah snorted. "Oh, yeah. I have a malfunctioning ventilation system he can fix."

"And Roth collected data on this Enclave with that mini-drone you gave him."

That made Noah sit up. He'd tweaked the mini-drone programming and wanted to see how much it had improved performance.

"Be at the debrief in thirty minutes," Elle added.

"See you there." Noah slid into his chair and as he did, his gaze caught on the stack of notes and blueprints in the center of his desk. Plans for Operation Swift Wind. He let out a long breath. There was a lot of work to do for the evac plan, and a hell of a lot of that work fell to him. They needed power, operational engines, illusion systems. He raked a hand through his hair. Pressure was a heavy load on his shoulders. The lives of hundreds of people depended on him.

Noah closed his eyes. Hell, he had more pressure now than when he'd run a million-dollar tech company. Everyone had wanted a piece of him then too. Well, his money anyway.

His ex-wife most of all. Nothing like realizing the woman who'd professed to love you loved your bank balance more.

In a way, he was thankful for the alien invasion.

It had stripped away the bullshit. People were their real selves. What car you drove, or clothes you wore, or how much money you had didn't matter anymore.

He reached back and grabbed a pair of dice off the shelf where his collection sat. His grandmother had been obsessed with her belief in luck. He rolled the small cubes between his fingers. She'd bought him his first set of dice when he was eight and he'd been collecting them ever since. He'd envied her that deep, abiding belief that selecting the right number, or positioning her furniture the right way would bring her luck in life.

Noah set the dice back on the shelf. He'd learned the hard way that Lady Luck was a bitch and you worked to make your own luck.

The comp lab door slammed open.

Captain Laura Bladon stood in the doorway—all neatly-pressed uniform, stern face and red hair tamed in a braid. Noah groaned. Captain Dragon had left her lair to breathe fire his way.

Her strides were stiff and her eyes were blazing. "The ventilation in the prison cells isn't working, Kim. And the comp system keeps freezing up. I need them fixed and you're in here daydreaming."

Noah counted to three. "No. I'm working." He waved at the whiteboard on the wall nearby listing all the tech team's jobs. "I've got comps to fix, an evac plan to work on, data from Masters to analyze. Get in line, Captain Dragon."

"Do not call me that. I have prisoners who need constraining and interrogating. I need our systems operational to do that."

God, his blood was boiling. This woman seemed capable of driving him to the edge with just a few words. "Like I said, get in line."

If her ears could steam, they would be now. Noah smothered a smile. Damn, he did enjoy riling her.

She was all spit and polish in those starched uniforms of hers. Such a contrast to the vibrant red of her hair. He wondered if she was as buttoned up underneath, or if there was fire simmering quietly.

That made Noah straighten like he'd gotten an electric shock. He had no interest in getting burned by Laura Bladon, one way or another. Absolutely not.

She slapped her palms on his desk. "Fix my comp system, Kim." She spun on her polished boots and strode out.

Noah looked at the door, then the work on his desk before tipping his head back to stare at the ceiling. Yep, Lady Luck just loved seeing him suffer.

***

"So Howell's dead," General Holmes said.

"Yes, sir." Roth stood, his hands resting in the small of his back as he finished debriefing the general. Beside him, he could see Avery wilting before his eyes. They needed a shower and bed. Soon.

In the corner of the conference room, Bastian

was curled up in a chair, asleep. Roth had already asked Arden to get Santha and her team to check if they'd ever run across the boy's parents.

"Howell was taken by the alien bugs," Avery said. "We tried to stop them...I mean, he wasn't a good man, but I don't think anyone deserves that."

Roth saw the flash of pain in her face. Knew she was thinking of Howell's kids.

"You're too kind, Avery," Marcus growled. "I say the man got exactly what he deserved."

"The leaders of the Enclave, Ivanov and Captain Scott, said we're welcome if we need somewhere to go," Roth added.

"Is it a viable option?" the general asked.

Roth nodded. "They're well set up. Sunlight system, decorated tunnels, large living quarters, and they have this area they call the Garden."

"It's open to the air, at the top of the escarpment and protected by an illusion system," Avery said. "Vegetable gardens, trees, flowers. It's beautiful."

"I used the mini-drone to collect data." Roth held out his tablet and turned to Noah sitting at the conference table. "Figured you'd like this."

Noah took it with a nod. "I'll pull all the data off and see what we can see. How'd the mini-drone do?"

"Whatever tweaks you did, it worked perfectly." Roth turned back to the others. "Howell was running the place with a mix of fear and benevolence. I think Ivanov and Scott will do a better job. If we have to evac there, it might be a tight squeeze, but it'd be doable."

The general sank back in his chair. "That's if we can even get there."

They were all silent. Roth knew moving almost a thousand people hundreds of kilometers while being hunted by aliens wouldn't be easy.

"I've stepped up preparations on Operation Swift Wind." Holmes rubbed the frown line between his eyebrows. "We're still sourcing and outfitting vehicles. And our first evacuation drill is tomorrow. I want everyone ready, in case we have to leave."

"I really, really hope the aliens don't attack," Avery said. "We might catch a break."

Roth hoped that was true, but he had that prickle at the back of his neck. That one he got whenever a mission was about to go bad.

Holmes nodded, his eyes looking incredibly old. "Let's hope so, but we'll be ready if they do."

Suddenly, the door slammed open and a wild-eyed woman with dark hair raced in. A tall man appeared behind her, his gaze searching the room.

They both spied the sleeping boy at the same moment. "Bastian!" the woman cried.

Roth's heart clenched and Avery grabbed his hand. They watched Bastian blink awake and then spot the couple. He froze, his face crumpling. "Mum? Dad?"

The couple moved, but Bastian was faster. He flew toward them and launched himself into their arms.

God, it looked like the kid had received a miracle. Roth smiled, and Avery leaned her head into him. He would have given his soul to have his parents and Gwen back. He looked around the room and damned if even Marcus didn't look moved by the sight of the sobbing boy and his parents.

Santha appeared in the doorway, her dark hair tied back in a ponytail. She spied the family and smiled. "I see they found him. They only arrived here a day ago. They've been resting and I was planning to debrief them on where they'd come from, and what they'd seen."

Roth nodded. "They might have more useful information on the Enclave." He watched the couple hugging Bastian hard. He understood how important it was to hold onto your loved ones and never let them go. "But let's give them some time first." Roth cleared his throat. "Sir, Avery and I have had a really long twenty-four hours."

Holmes waved his hand. "Go. Get some rest."

Rest was on the list, but so were a few other items. Getting Avery under him again was one of them.

And convincing her he really was falling in love with her, and to take a risk and be his was another.

As he followed her out of the conference room, he wondered if facing down aliens might be an easier task.

***

"Roth, I'm almost there. Don't stop."

Avery gripped Roth's shoulders as he pinned her against the tiles in his small shower. His cock was already lodged deep inside her and he was moving hard and fast.

The water pounded over them and Avery was lost in the rush of sensations. Roth's hard body, the warm water, the cool tiles and the hammering of his heart where his chest was pressed to hers.

Another thrust and her orgasm ripped through her. She screamed his name, and a second later, he thrust deep and held himself there as he came.

Spent, she dropped her head to his shoulder. She was dimly aware of him turning the shower off and carrying her to the bed.

He sat down, lay back, and pulled her on top of him. She settled in. She could definitely get used to using him as her personal pillow. She'd always thought she loved sleeping alone, but Roth was proving her wrong.

A hand stroked through her hair, and she pressed her lips to his neck. Lazily, she nipped at him.

"Hey, no hickeys." With his other hand, he swatted her butt. The gentle slap turned into a caress. "You're mine, Avery. You've accused me of macho alpha male shit…and I am an alpha male." A fierce growl. "That means I'm not letting you go. No matter what."

Her pulse doubled its pace. She'd never been in love before, but she guessed this breathless, scary, elated feeling she felt when she looked at Roth was it. She admired his strength, his dedication, and she wanted to see him safe and happy.

"I'm afraid to love you," she whispered. "What if I lose you?"

"Hey." He tugged her head up, so his ice-colored eyes were on hers. "There are no guarantees, sweetheart. Especially in this changed world we live in. But I think it makes it even more important to find the things that matter, and hold on to them real tight." He cupped her cheek. "I know what it is to lose everything. But I would never trade my time with my family in order to avoid the pain of losing them." He rubbed his thumb over her lips. "I'm not planning on going anywhere, and knowing you're here, making my life that little bit better, that'll make me fight harder, smarter."

"God, Roth." She covered his hand with hers.

"And I'm guessing you'll want to join the squads, now that you've got the medical all-clear." He smiled. "No more peeling potatoes."

"Chef will not be happy." The humor drained away. "I'm actually thinking I'll join Santha's recon team. With her expecting a baby, Devlin's taking on more work. They could use my skills."

"Hell, yeah," Roth agreed.

God, the man was perfect. That feeling inside swelled, filling her chest. "I'm so afraid to lose you, but I love you anyway."

Pleasure flared in his eyes. "I love you, Avery. I love your fight, your fierceness." He took her mouth, drinking deep. He pulled back and pressed his nose to hers. "I love that you take action, even when you're afraid. And I want to be by your side. Always."

"How can you love like that? So fearlessly?"

"I'm afraid too, sweetheart. Losing my family

almost killed me. But I have my squad, my friends...I have you. My family gave me the foundation to care for others."

Avery felt her stomach harden. "I don't have that foundation, Roth. I never had anything like that."

He pressed a gentle kiss to her lips. "Then let me be your foundation. We'll work it out together."

"You're on." She nuzzled into him. "We still need to throw that laser ball around. I know I can take you down."

"Sweetheart, there's no way."

She narrowed her gaze and sat up, straddling his hard body. "Oh? Well, how about another challenge first?" She scooted back and walked her fingers down the center of his chest. "First one to make the other orgasm wins."

He raised a brow. "You're on. What's the prize?"

"An orgasm."

Roth laughed, and it brought the brightest joy to her. A joy she wasn't sure she'd ever felt. With the man she loved by her side, she knew they could face anything. "I've got you, Roth Masters."

He reared up, wrapping his arms around her. "No, sweetheart, we've got each other. Always."

I hope you enjoyed Roth and Avery's story!

Hell Squad continues with NOAH, the story of tech genius, Noah Kim, and Captain Laura Bladon. Read on for a preview.

Don't miss out! For updates about new releases, action romance info, free books, and other fun stuff, sign up for my VIP mailing list and get your *free box set* containing three action-packed romances.

Visit here to get started:
www.annahackettbooks.com

FREE BOX SET DOWNLOAD

JOIN THE ACTION-PACKED ADVENTURE!

Formats: Kindle, ePub, PDF

Preview – Hell Squad: Noah

One job down. Five hundred and seven to go.

Noah Kim ducked out of the small doorway and into the bright afternoon sun. He pressed a hidden button on the outside and watched the door—camouflaged to look like rock—slide closed. Once it was shut, there was no way to tell a secret entrance was hidden there.

He turned and started walking into the trees, headed back to Blue Mountain Base.

The secret storage facility he was working in was a ten minute walk from the main base. When they'd turned the former military base into a haven for survivors of the vicious alien invasion that had decimated Earth a year and a half ago, none of them had known this secret storage area was here.

Noah had discovered it when he and his tech team had been busy upgrading a part of the power system. He'd stumbled across old electrical cables that led in this direction from the main base. From what he could tell, the facility had housed some sort of power generator, as there were still giant turbines in place, but over the years—as energy technology increased and nuclear generators had become safe and solar-power systems viable—it had become obsolete.

The best thing about it, though, was the facility wasn't listed on Blue Mountain Base's official plans. Plans they'd recently discovered the leader of the United Coalition of Countries had sold to the aliens in return for his own safety.

Noah scowled. *Bastard.* President Howell had saved himself, and not the millions of people he'd vowed to protect. Noah stopped, forcing himself to take a second to breathe in the fresh mountain air to calm his temper. Summer was approaching, and temperatures were beginning to rise. In fact, the afternoon was hot.

Right here, right now, surrounded by the tall gum trees and hearing the rustle of small animals in the bushes and the sounds of birds overhead, Noah could almost pretend the invasion had never happened. That the dinosaur-like raptors had never arrived in their monstrous, giant spaceships and wiped out all the major cities on the planet. His gaze turned to the east, but the view was blocked by the trees. Still, he knew the ruins of Sydney were there—the once-beautiful, busy capital of the Coalition. Now, nothing more than a broken, deserted ruin.

One of those shattered skyscrapers had housed Noah's billion-dollar, online tech company. He'd always loved electronics, from the time he was old enough to tap on a comp. He'd driven his parents crazy, tinkering with things. At the age of five, he'd freaked his mother out by disassembling the toaster because it kept burning his toast. After he'd put it back together, it had worked like new. At ten, he'd pulled his father's comp apart. Noah had inherited his father's short temper. But after a fiery outburst, and after Noah added a few improvements and reassembled the comp, his dad had loved his faster device.

Noah had started work in a private R and D company in his teens, making a small fortune in salary. Then he'd started his own company, made his first million at seventeen, and his first billion at twenty-five. Kim Technology Inc. had been known as a hip, creative place to work, and a place on the cutting edge of tech. He'd been inundated by bright, young grads looking for work. Some days, he'd wished he wasn't the boss. Some days he hadn't wanted all the calls, emails, and meetings—he'd just wanted to lock himself in his tech lab and fiddle with his latest ideas.

Well, now he got to hang out in his tech lab all the time. There wasn't a whole hell of a lot of tinkering now, though. Mostly he kept the base's ventilation running, the lights on, and the hot water hot, and fixed every other damn problem the residents had. He started walking again, scraping a hand through his straight, black hair. It had gotten so long, it brushed his shoulders, something that would have given his old-fashioned grandmother heart failure.

The thought of her made him smile, and a small pain burned in his heart. God, he missed her and his parents. His Aussie mother and South Korean father had been on a vacation in South Korea, visiting his grandmother, when the aliens invaded. Some small part of him hoped they'd survived, but Seoul had been wiped out, just like every other major city around the world.

He rounded a tree and kept moving. He never used the same path to the storage facility twice. Devlin, second-in-command of the base's recon team, had scouted out a few different routes with him. Dev had warned that they couldn't risk leaving a trail the aliens could spot.

In the storage facility was the base's last hope if the aliens found them.

General Adam Holmes, head of Blue Mountain Base, was working overtime with Noah to get Operation Swift Wind organized. They had to get it operational *before* the aliens attacked.

And everyone knew it was only a matter of time.

Noah stepped into a clearing, taking a second to enjoy the sun—he missed it, being stuck underground. He might love being hunched over a desk with electronic components spread in front of him, but he'd also been a keen surfer. Bondi Beach had been a favorite place of his to escape to on the weekends.

Needless to say, he didn't get to surf anymore.

Suddenly, there was a loud rushing noise in the sky. Frowning, he glanced up—and saw a small raptor ptero ship whizz by overhead.

Fucking hell. He froze. What were they doing so close to base?

Another flew past. Its shape was so distinctive—

like the flying dinosaurs of Earth's past, it had two large wings, and narrowed into points at both the front and back. Red lights glowed along the wings and what had to be the cockpit window at the front.

Fear spurred him to action, and Noah started to run. He glimpsed the pteros wheeling around, pointed wings aimed at the ground as they executed impossibly tight turns. Apparently, it had been too much to hope that they hadn't seen him.

Shit.

They flew straight back in his direction.

Noah pumped his arms, his heart thumping in his chest. He went to the gym, kept fit. But deep down, he knew he couldn't cross the clearing in time.

Green poison splattered the ground around him. He skidded to a halt, dirt flying, and dodged to the side.

Frantically, he checked he hadn't been hit. Nearby, he heard the sizzle as the raptor poison ate through the grass and dirt. He knew the stuff paralyzed, and apparently hurt like hell. He ran again, pushing for all the speed he had. He glanced back and saw the ships turning again for another pass. *Shit, shit, shit.*

Suddenly, people poured out of the trees. Soldiers dressed in black carbon fiber armor.

"Noah!" Marcus Steele yelled. "Get down."

Noah dropped.

Marcus was leader of the base's roughest, toughest group of commandos—Hell Squad. The rest of Hell Squad's soldiers fanned out. They were all holding their carbines, aiming into the sky. One of them, Reed MacKinnon, held a modified carbine Noah knew could also fire explosives.

And the squad's sniper, Shaw Baird, was balancing a laser-guided missile launcher on his shoulder. The squad's only female soldier, Claudia Frost, stood beside him, her laser scope held up as she targeted the enemy.

"Steady," she said. "Steady. Fire!"

Shaw fired the rocket launcher. The missile launched, Shaw absorbing the recoil. The rest of the squad members were firing their carbines.

Noah couldn't stop himself, he looked back over his shoulder.

The missile flew straight and slammed into the lead ptero.

It exploded in a ball of flames.

Noah held his arm up to shield his face from the huge explosion. The second ptero peeled away and, quick as lightning, disappeared.

Noah released a shaky breath. *Hell.*

"Okay?" Cruz Ramos, Hell Squad's second-in-command stood above Noah offering him a hand.

He took it and got to his feet. "Yeah. Glad you guys arrived when you did."

"We're on base patrol today. Elle saw the damn things zipping in."

Elle was their comms officer. Noah knew she was in the base somewhere, monitoring drone feed and providing her squad with intel.

The rest of the squad strolled forward, their largest, quietest and deadliest soldier, Gabe, bringing up the rear.

"That was closer than we've ever seen them," Marcus said.

"Hell, that was too damn close." Shaw set the missile launcher down.

They all stared at the beautiful blue sky.

"Yeah," Noah answered. He felt a heavy weight settle on his shoulders. He had to get the kinks ironed out of Operation Swift Wind...because right now, if they had to evacuate, they wouldn't make it.

"How's the Swift Wind convoy going?" Marcus asked, as though the man had read Noah's mind.

Noah shrugged. "We have a pretty motley collection of vehicles for the convoy. I've retrofitted all of them with small nuclear reactors, so they have power."

Shaw pulled a face. "Why do I hear a huge *but* in your voice?"

"They'll run, but I can't hide them."

The Hell Squad soldiers were all quiet, their faces grim.

"Can't you put illusion systems on them?" Reed, a former Coalition Navy SEAL, asked.

Noah wished. Illusion systems provided a cloak—messed with a vehicle's signature on raptor scans, blurred it from sight, and used directed sound waves to distort any noise. He shook his head. "I don't have the parts to outfit every vehicle with its own illusion system."

"Shit," mumbled Claudia.

Yeah, because if even one vehicle was visible and they were running from the aliens, one vehicle would be enough for the enemy to pinpoint their location.

Noah rubbed the back of his neck. "I'm working on an illusion system to cover the entire convoy."

"I take it that it would need to be a large system," Marcus said.

"Yes. And right now, I can't power it."

"Not even with a nuclear reactor?" Cruz's voice held a Mexican accent.

"No. It's complicated—"

Shaw leaned close to Claudia. "That means he thinks we're dumb."

Noah shook his head. "A large-scale illusion system seems to cause nuclear reactor instability."

Reed shifted. "What about the alien power cubes?"

Reed's fiancée, Dr. Natalya Vasin, was a brilliant energy scientist who had been helping unravel the mystery of the alien energy cubes they'd liberated from the raptors.

"They don't interface easily with our tech. Natalya's been helping, but while we can activate the cubes, pull them apart, and put them back together, we can't seem to use the cubes to power our stuff reliably."

"Damn," Reed muttered.

Damn was right. Noah felt that crushing weight again. The survival of every man, woman, and child in the base was his responsibility.

And he was failing them. He had to get this right, or people would die.

As he followed the others back to Blue Mountain

Base, those words kept thumping in his head. But once he got back to the comp lab, the massive pile of work waiting for him provided a much-needed distraction. He could think more about the power problem later. For the moment, he rolled up his sleeves and got busy.

Almost got it. Noah leaned over his battered desk, hand holding the tiny comp chip he'd just fixed steady as he inserted it back into the comp. Delicate work, but he'd always had steady hands.

Just as he maneuvered the chip into its slot, an alarm started blaring.

Noah jerked, the chip flew out of his tweezers, hit the floor and skittered under the neighboring desk.

He sucked in a breath, and closed his eyes. *Count to three, Kim.*

Finally, he opened his eyes and pulled his glasses off—he only needed the damn things when his eyes were tired. He stared at the orange light flashing above the door. He'd known the evacuation drill was happening this evening...he'd just lost track of time.

He pushed his chair back, then went looking for his missing chip.

Noah knew the drill was important. If the damned aliens invaded the base, they had to be ready to leave. He just wished they had a protected convoy to leave in.

The comp lab was empty, most of his tech team out fixing various things around the underground base. He reached under the desk, searching for the chip. Yep, this was definitely a far cry from his millionaire existence before the alien invasion.

He thought of his parents again. The last time he'd seen them, they'd fought. He'd been off the rails a little, rolling in money and prestige. Yeah, maybe he'd let it all go to his head.

He'd had a collection of expensive sports cars, a fancy penthouse apartment in the city, and had always been at the latest parties and hottest nightclubs. And after the hell Kalina had put him through, he'd worked his way through a long list of glamorous party girls.

His father had been trying to get him to wake up and focus on what really mattered.

"Well, Dad, your pep talk didn't work, but the alien invasion certainly did the trick." Noah cursed, maneuvering his arm awkwardly until his fingers closed over the chip. Exhaling loudly, he went back to his desk and finally got the chip in place.

He glanced up, and the small glowing cube and bits of alien tech on the corner of his desk snagged his attention. And made his jaw tighten.

The lab door slammed open and Roth Masters—leader of Squad Nine—stood in the doorway.

"Kim, alarm means you evacuate." The man was tall and built big. He had a rugged face and ice-blue eyes, and could look pretty intimidating.

Noah had never let anyone intimidate him. "Got work to do, Roth. It's only a drill."

"Yeah, and everyone needs to have this down pat in case it turns into the real thing."

Noah scowled and waved at the tech on his desk.

"If I don't get this work done, there won't be anywhere for people to evacuate to."

Roth blew out a breath and nodded. "Marcus told me you're working on power for the illusion system for the Swift Wind convoy."

"Yeah."

"No luck?"

Luck. There was a concept Noah thought about a lot. He reached back and snagged a couple of his dice off the shelf behind him. One was red with white dots, the other a shiny, metallic silver. He had an entire collection of them—of all shapes, sizes and materials—although it was only a small portion of what he'd owned before. These were all he'd managed to save.

"Not yet." Lady Luck was being pretty stingy with him lately.

Roth's gaze landed on the alien cube. "You trying to use the alien energy cubes?"

"No, Masters, I hadn't thought of that." When the soldier lifted a brow, Noah sighed and sank back in his chair. "Sorry. We're working on it, but it seems like everyone needs something these days."

Yep, everyone wanted a piece of him. Some days it felt like he was back at his tech company, where he had accountants to hassle him with budgets, his management team with some new strategy, and tech geeks who wanted jobs, or for him to endorse their latest invention. Oh, and the people who'd wanted money. Women who'd wanted money. Just like his fucking ex-wife.

Roth grinned. "I could always use more tech to

test in the field. Marcus keeps riding me about the fact he never gets any of the good stuff you cook up." The man's grin widened. "I'd like to keep bugging him."

Noah snorted. He knew the rivalry between the squads was all in good fun. "Get in line, Roth. I have comps in the schoolrooms to repair, the Swift Wind convoy to work on, and the ventilation's playing up in sector four." A ping came from Noah's comp. He glanced at the screen and when he saw the message, he rolled his eyes. "Oh, and now Captain Dragon has damn well broken the comp in the prison area...again."

Roth lifted a brow. "Captain Dragon?"

"Bladon." Captain Laura Bladon ran the prison area and interrogation team with a damn iron fist. Every time he had the misfortune to step foot in there, she made his life hell. She lived and breathed her work—one of the few things he found admirable about her. She wanted to beat the aliens, no matter what the cost, and that was great—but damn, she needed to loosen up. "I reckon if she could breathe fire, she would."

Roth's lips twitched. "It would match her hair."

That it would. An image of Laura's vibrant red hair flashed in his eyes. She kept it tightly braided, but even when she was nagging him to get her comp system fixed, he wondered what it would look like left loose and falling around her shoulders.

The alarm that had been shrilly blaring suddenly cut off. The silence was deafening.

"Guess the drill's over," Noah said.

"Yeah." Roth glanced at his watch. "I need to go and debrief on the evac. Next time, can you play nice and at least make it look like you're evacuating?"

"Don't hold your breath."

Roth shook his head. "Avery wants to have a few people over for dinner some time. Squad Nine, Hell Squad, you. I think she and Elle have it in their heads you've been working too hard and need to chill out."

Avery Stillman was a former Coalition Central Intelligence Agent. She'd been rescued from a tank in an alien lab and had helped Roth uncover some secrets about the aliens. And in the process, they'd fallen in love. They'd also recently discovered another secret human enclave, hidden underground not far from Blue Mountain Base. A viable, alternative place for them to go if they were attacked.

And sweet Elle Milton was Noah's friend. Noah liked her a lot, had even briefly considered dipping back into the relationship waters for her...but Elle had only ever had eyes for Marcus. Everyone in base was still shaking their heads over the former socialite and the scarred soldier—beauty and the beast.

"Sounds good," Noah said.

But as Roth left, Noah stared at the man's back. They fit, Roth and Avery. Elle and Marcus. They made each other happy and found their own little piece of heaven in the middle of hell. Noah's hand tightened on the edge of his desk. Hell, before the alien invasion, he hadn't believed in connections like that. But each couple had gotten lucky.

Noah lifted the dice, turning them over in his hands. Luck was a capricious bitch, that was for sure. She blessed some and cursed others.

His comp pinged again, and he saw another more insistent message from Captain Dragon. With a grin, he flicked his screen off. That was one thing he'd learned since the apocalypse—you had to enjoy the small pleasures, wherever you could find them.

Hell Squad

Marcus
Cruz
Gabe
Reed
Roth
Noah
Shaw
Holmes

MORE ACTION ROMANCE?

**ACTION
ADVENTURE
TREASURE HUNTS
SEXY SCI-FI ROMANCE**

When astro-archeologist and museum curator Dr. Lexa Carter discovers a secret map to a lost old Earth treasure—a priceless Fabergé egg—she's excited at the prospect of a treasure hunt to the dangerous desert planet of Zerzura. What she's not so happy about is being saddled with a bodyguard—the museum's mysterious new head of security, Damon Malik.

After many dangerous years as a galactic spy, Damon Malik just wanted a quiet job where no one tried to kill him. Instead of easy work in a museum full of artifacts, he finds himself on a backwater planet babysitting the most infuriating woman he's ever met.

She thinks he's arrogant. He thinks she's a trouble-magnet. But among the desert sands and ruins, adventure led by a young, brash treasure hunter named Dathan Phoenix, takes a deadly turn. As it becomes clear that someone doesn't want them to find the treasure, Lexa and Damon will have to trust each other just to survive.

The Phoenix Adventures

Among Galactic Ruins
At Star's End
In the Devil's Nebula
On a Rogue Planet
Beneath a Trojan Moon
Beyond Galaxy's Edge
On a Cyborg Planet
Return to Dark Earth
On a Barbarian World

Also by Anna Hackett

Hell Squad
Marcus
Cruz
Gabe
Reed
Roth
Noah
Shaw
Holmes

The Anomaly Series
Time Thief
Mind Raider
Soul Stealer
Salvation
Anomaly Series Box Set

The Phoenix Adventures
Among Galactic Ruins
At Star's End
In the Devil's Nebula
On a Rogue Planet
Beneath a Trojan Moon
Beyond Galaxy's Edge
On a Cyborg Planet
Return to Dark Earth
On a Barbarian World

Perma Series
Winter Fusion
The WindKeepers Series
Wind Kissed, Fire Bound
Taken by the South Wind
Tempting the West Wind
Defying the North Wind
Claiming the East Wind

Standalone Titles
Savage Dragon
Hunter's Surrender
One Night with the Wolf

Anthologies
A Galactic Holiday
Moonlight (UK only)
Vampire Hunter (UK only)
Awakening the Dragon (UK Only)

About the Author

I'm a USA Today bestselling author and I'm passionate about *action romance*. I love stories that combine the thrill of falling in love with the excitement of action, danger and adventure. I'm a sucker for that moment when the team is walking in slow motion, shoulder-to-shoulder heading off into battle.

I write about people overcoming unbeatable odds and achieving seemingly impossible goals. I like to believe it's possible for all of us to do the same.

My books are mixture of action, adventure and sexy romance and they're recommended for anyone who enjoys fast-paced stories where the boy wins the girl at the end (or sometimes the girl wins the boy!)

For release dates, action romance info, free books, and other fun stuff, sign up for the latest news here:

Website: AnnaHackettBooks.com

Printed in Great Britain
by Amazon

36185851R00135